RETURN TO CANTA LUPE

RETURN TO CANTA LUPE

THOMAS JEIER
and
JEFFREY M. WALLMANN

DOUBLEDAY & COMPANY, INC.
GARDEN CITY, NEW YORK
1983

All of the characters in this book are fictitious, and any resemblance to actual persons, living or dead, is purely coincidental.

CIP Data Applied For
Library of Congress Catalog Card Number 82-45327

Printed in the United States of America

RETURN TO CANTA LUPE

CHAPTER 1

The storm that had been mildly threatening since mid-morning came with stunning swiftness. One moment the afternoon was sunlit through a diffusion of clouds, the next it was dark and ominous.

Matt Bishop shifted moodily in his saddle and wedged his worn Stetson more firmly on his head. His wrinkled shirttail flapping in the rising breeze attested to the fact that he had been riding for quite some time and had often hunched his shoulders. A six-footer and whipcord lean despite a voracious appetite, Bishop was wrinkled and weathered by the passing of some two score in the saddle. He had a drawn, horsey face, deeply lined around brown basset eyes; and though his hair was as thick as ever, it had turned salt-and-pepperish with the years, as had his untrimmed bandido moustache, which drooped on either side of his thin-lipped, tobacco-stained mouth.

The breeze quickened, portending worse. Bishop reached behind and was tucking in his shirttail when the rain began, fat and heavy. He reined in, got his cracked yellow slicker out of his war bag and put it on, then jiggered his horse moving again, all the while cussing around the two-a-penny, "short six" cigar clamped in his teeth. Goddamn Kansas. By all rights, he should be in goddamn Arizona or New Mexico, where it was warm and sunshiny even in goddamn November, instead of up in this miserable mud-puddle region. But it couldn't be helped. The newspaper story had already been a couple of months old when he'd chanced upon it last week, and if he'd waited any longer—

say, until spring—the trail would've probably become too cold to follow.

The storm increased with a churning force, the wind swirling in from the north now and pushing the rains ahead of it in chilling, boisterous swells. Bishop bent his head against the buffeting wind, the brim of his hat acting like a rain gutter pouring a continuous stream of water almost in his lap. More water seeped in through the openings of his slicker, soaking him to the skin, and with it came the wind, setting up a piercing, cold ache in his bones.

Bishop grimaced in pain, the rheumatism which had been pestering for the past several years flaring up again in the joints of his arms and legs. When he got to hurting this bad, it was about all he could manage to just hang on and let his horse find its own way.

This time, at least, it was a relatively safe thing for Bishop to do. His chestnut gelding couldn't wander far afield or seek shelter from the downpour because the road was lined on both sides by endless barbed-wire fences. And damn these goddamn wire fences too, Bishop thought savagely. Back in the old days, folks would've never dreamed of butchering the rangeland into parcels, back then when a man was free to move whenever and wherever he saw fit.

He canted his hat at a better angle to the rain and allowed himself to indulge in rather rosy reminiscences of the old days. Many were hazy memories of people and places long since gone, but others were of a more recent nature, such as those of eating. Food was one of Bishop's favorite subjects, so for some while he slogged along, basking wistfully in recollections of steaks and taters and deep-dish apple pies he'd once known and loved. Unfortunately, his entire bankroll consisted of one dollar and thirty cents, so he doubted he'd soon have the chance to catch up on his dream. Then again, perhaps when he reached Sugarwood he'd be lucky and find a job. Problem was, he couldn't get along at all with clodhopping farmers, and no rancher in his right mind would give him work as a wrangler or puncher anymore, considering his age. Ah well, maybe he could wangle a spot sweeping out a livery stable or swamping in a saloon or washing dishes in a restaurant. That would be the job to try for—the pay would be lousy, but restaurants usually threw in meals.

The road veered away from the flat prairie and climbed a low, crumbly-faced butte. On the other side, it meandered through a patch of tall boulders, and it was just beyond them that Bishop glimpsed Sugarwood emerging out of the gloom and driving sheets of rain.

There was not, he thought, a helluva lot to see.

The town was a farm hamlet, huddling with a few trees along the bank of a small river and lying smack-dab athwart a railroad track. The railroad track ran in an absolutely straight east-west course, appearing to Bishop as if it came out of nowhere on his right, crossed the river on a trestle, then vanished just as swiftly on his left—and, in the process, sliced through the middle of Sugarwood like a hot wire through cheese. And, when Bishop finally reached the town limits, he discovered the trail became the main—and only—street, which some patriotic idiot had christened Theodore Roosevelt Boulevard.

Due to the rain, the boulevard resembled a plowed trench of gumbo. Flanking it were a half-dozen or so false-fronted buildings—only the hotel had a true second floor—and about an equal number of warped frame houses. Behind them lay broken-fenced corrals, pig wallows, and empty lots littered with garbage. Farther along were the bisecting tracks, and a depot and telegrapher's office, and beyond them the town petered out into boxlike cabins and swaybacked sheds sagging away from the prevailing wind.

Bishop spat out his now soggy and utterly ruined cigar. "If Teddy had ever laid eyes on this place," he muttered to himself, "he'd have stayed in Cuba with his Rough Riders, I betcha."

Actually, Bishop had visited hundreds of towns as sorry as Sugarwood and hadn't found them particularly repulsive. The last town he'd passed through and the one before it had been even worse, yet he'd cared so little that he couldn't be bothered to remember their names. But with Sugarwood it was different. He'd been obsessed with this central Kansan flyspeck ever since he'd read about it back in Dodge City. Purely by accident, too: a baker had wrapped some biscuits for him in an old page of the *Times,* and Bishop had idly scanned the newspage that night, not having anything else to look at.

Sugarwood in itself had meant nothing; it was what had happened here which had perked Bishop's interest. According to the three-column report, Timotheus Tighe, the Hodgeman County deputy sheriff stationed in Sugarwood, had single-handedly captured two Leavenworth escapees. This was especially noteworthy, because while the prisoners were both young, brutish killers, Deputy Tighe was seventy-two years old, and weighed all of a hundred and forty pounds with his boots on.

Timotheus Tighe!

The *Times* reporter, Bishop realized, had not done his homework. If he had, he'd have fleshed out the article with an account of Tighe's remarkable history as a lawman. For almost half a century, Timotheus Tighe had been actively pursuing outlaws, either as a bounty hunter or a badge-toter, and at times when he could get away with it, as both at the same time. Tighe had a well-earned reputation for being tenacious and ruthless and downright devious when necessary; and, as he'd often bragged, he had a record of always bringing in his man.

Well, almost always.

Not that Tighe ever volunteered to admit his only four failures—the four amateur bandits who'd robbed the Canta Lupe Bank & Trust in broad daylight. And not that Tighe hadn't tried to catch them—indeed, he'd never given up, not even after the statute of limitations had run out and everybody else had long forgotten about the whole thing. And not that Tighe didn't know who the four were—Harold Shelby, the greedy dreamer who'd first thought of the caper; Emmett Crandon, the semipro gambler who'd craftily plotted the operation; Guffy LeRoy, the hell-raising, spoiled rich kid who'd dared them to try it; and

Matthew Bishop, the drifting cowboy who'd had nothing better to do right then.

Bishop smiled wryly as he recalled the robbery. Unlike Sugarwood, Canta Lupe was a boom town situated in Arizona's silver region, near the Mexican border. The bank was owned by a skinflint bastard who'd steal the blanket out of his mother's kennel, and they'd all been taken by him at one time or another, and it didn't take much prodding to decide to shake him down to his bones. Eagerly they cased the bank for a week. Then on a Monday in October of 1887, they walked in with big-bore scatter-guns and walked out with the two hundred thousand dollars the local mines had just deposited for their payrolls. It was a breeze, simply in and out, and then a wild gallop toward Mexico.

Within minutes a posse was pounding after them. It was led by Tighe, who at the time was a special marshal appointed by the mineowners to protect their shipments, including the payrolls. So even though his official capacity ended at the bank, and he was not held responsible in the least, he still took the robbery as a personal affront.

After Tighe and his posse returned empty-handed, the mineowners posted a fat reward. A whole slew of sheriffs, Arizona Rangers, bounty hunters, and even Indians began combing the Southwest, some of them moving as far south as Veracruz in hopes of a lead. Their searching was futile, because the robbers never went south, the way it was logically supposed, the way they made it appear they had. Instead, the four had circled around Canta Lupe and had gone northeastward, crossing the Gallina Mountains, bypassing Albuquerque, and striking up through Colorado into Nebraska.

Eventually, of course, the pursuers grew wise to the trick. But by then the four had split up, with Emmett Crandon, the planner and detail man, having already made sure each of their trails was well masked. So after a while longer of fruitless searching, the badge-toters and headhunters went back to easier pursuits, most of them not having any jurisdiction outside their immediate territory anyway; and besides, insurance had covered the stolen wages, and the mineowners had disgustedly withdrawn their reward offer. So what the hell, why break your ass over a hard-rock nothing?

Timotheus Tighe, however, did not stop. He continued to break his ass, the passage of years seeming to crystallize his determination to catch them. True, he couldn't devote himself entirely to them. He had other duties to perform, other crooks to run down. But whenever he had the chance, he'd stubbornly scratch for clues and dig around old traces, and occasionally had come close to snagging one or another of them, sometimes missing them only by hours, only by bad luck. Nevertheless, it remained that after twenty-five years of dogging them, he still hadn't caught up with the nose-thumbing robbers.

Naturally, Bishop was aware that Tighe was after him. And though he hadn't seen the other three since the holdup, he was sure they also knew what Tighe was up to and were taking precautions, else he'd have learned of their capture. He himself didn't feel especially threatened, because he'd never stuck in one place long enough to grow roots and allow Tighe to catch up. Bishop was still fiddle-footed, his share of the loot having been quickly frittered away on women and booze, and mostly on friends who could never quite pay him back. But to Bishop, friendship was right up there in importance with eating, because, with a guy like him, they were about the only two things he felt he could hang onto that were worth a good goddamn.

So it wasn't surprising that after all these years together, he'd grown to enjoy Tighe's persistent hunt, and he would have missed the challenge, the spice, if Tighe were to ever call it off. It was as though Tighe had become a strange sort of invisible companion, one in which Bishop could take a vaguely affectionate interest. He could even sympathize with Tighe, understanding how this blot on an otherwise unblemished record must gall the old lawman, must goad him almost to insanity. And whenever a long stretch of time passed without news about

Tighe, Bishop even found himself wondering if he was alright, or if he was sick or injured or in some kind of trouble.

This last period of silence had been the longest. When Bishop happened across the newspaper story, he'd spent the night arguing with himself over what, if anything, to do about it. By morning, his curiosity had gotten the better of his caution. He'd set off to learn why Tighe would become a lowly deputy in a pissant burg like Sugarwood. Had Tighe stumbled onto a lead to one of the others, or had he finally given up and settled there to retire? The article didn't make it sound as if Tighe had grown too old or feeble to wear a badge, and yet . . .

What it came down to, Bishop had to admit, was that he himself had reached that age when he had more past than future. He was being prompted by nostalgia, much as Tighe was motivated by pride. And besides, he had nothing better to do right now. . . .

So now he was in Sugarwood, with few plans, little money, and no hope of evading Tighe if Tighe were to recognize who he was.

Some of the buildings and homes had lantern-lit windows, but there was no one in sight on or off the street. But that was not unusual, considering the size of the town and the foul weather. Bishop looked about for his most pressing needs—quarters for his horse and for himself. He saw a livery stable on his right and rode straight in. The stable appeared to be empty, but the hostler couldn't have gone far, for a small forge was still glowing and a horseshoe lay on the anvil.

"Hey!" Bishop called out. "Anybody here?"

No answer.

"Hey, c'mon!" he yelled louder. "You want my business or not?"

He waited, but there was still no reply. Dismounting, he began unsaddling his horse and cursing the hostler, whom he suspected was in the saloon, washing down the acrid stench and heat of the forge.

He brushed the gelding and led it to a vacant stall, where he tossed in some feed he dug out of the hostler's bins. He took his time about it, but he was still alone by the time he was through.

He started to leave, pausing at the stable entrance to eye the saloon across the street. It was then he realized just how silent Sugarwood was. The only sounds he could hear were the stabled horses nickering in their stalls and the morose wail of the storm sluicing through the street. It made him think of a ghost town, but that was nonsense. People had to be living here—lanterns were lit, the stable was open, horses and wagons were bogged in the mud alongside hitching rails, and the chimney above the saloon was belching wind-whipped swirls of smoke.

Bishop dashed across to the opposite boardwalk and tried the door of the saloon. It was locked. He pounded on the door and shouted, then waited a few minutes, but nobody came. He frowned. This was becoming downright weird. No saloon he'd ever heard of was closed at four in the afternoon—not short of a disaster.

The cafe next to the saloon was shuttered as well as locked. Bishop kept on rattling doorknobs and peering in windows, to no avail. He came to the hotel and, almost startled to find it open, went inside. The lobby was empty, as were the office and living quarters behind the front desk. He loped up the stairs to the second floor, but the rooms were either locked or vacant.

Going downstairs again, he went outside and yelled at the top of his voice, but there was still no response. A clammy sensation began creeping up between his shoulder blades. He drew his old Colt .44-40 Frontier, thinking to fire off a couple of shots, but then he reconsidered and holstered his revolver. Bullets were too expensive to waste, and he couldn't be sure he wouldn't be needing them later on.

He continued along the boardwalk, toward the depot. Just this side of the depot was a low, barn-size clapboard building; its fading whitewashed front had two of those churchlike arched windows, one on each side of a door with curtained glass panes. Above them ran a long sign reading: HUMMINGBIRD CHAPEL & MORTUARY, followed in smaller print by: *Weddings, Funerals, Services in Every Denomination.* And as Bishop drew closer to the Hummingbird Chapel, he realized that somebody inside it was playing "Nearer to Thee" on a pedal organ.

Stepping in, Bishop entered a small antechamber. There was a rolltop desk and chair, a filing cabinet, and a coffin of raw pine lumber standing upright in one corner, as if on display. An archway in the middle of the far wall was cloaked by thick blue velvet drapes. The organ music, louder now, was filtering out from the other side of the drapes, and now Bishop could detect the sound of a voice as well.

Bishop parted the drapes. They fell in place behind him, and he found himself in a large square room that served as the chapel. Seated on benches or folding chairs, facing a podium toward Bishop's left, was the population of Sugarwood. All hundred-and-whatever residents, or so it appeared to Bishop.

At one end of the podium, a wimpy, black-frocked man stood at a lectern, reading passages from a frayed Bible in a weak, syrupy voice. At the other end, a matronly woman was pumping the organ, playing much softer now, the music lacking any recognizable melody. In the center of the podium were four sawhorses, and balanced across two of them was a wooden casket painted green and sporting brass handles.

Instinctively Bishop yearned to leave, a part of his subconscious convinced that death was somehow a contagious disease. But he forced himself to stay, to move inconspicuously along the shadowy side wall until he was in a position to survey the congregation.

He was disappointed but not surprised when he failed to locate Tighe—or rather, an elderly man who'd look the way Tighe must by now. Bishop recalled what Tighe had looked like back at the time of the robbery: swarthy, medium-built, bowlegged enough to fork the stoutest of horses, and with a great fat nose that resembled the red squeeze bulb on a spray bottle. Age would have altered many things, but never those wishbone legs or that tomato of a beak.

"'Man that is born of woman hath but a short time to live, and is full of misery,'" droned the speaker—a minister, Bishop assumed, or perhaps a justice of the peace—and the organist kept noodling away in tuneless accompaniment. Bishop remained quiet in the gloom, another man among the mourners having caught his attention. The man was short, pudgy around the chest and belly, and appeared to be somewhere in his fifties. He was also bald, except for a pair of well-cultivated muttonchops. It was the bristly side-whiskers which held Bishop's interest; they struck a chord of familiarity, as did the man's deep-set onyx eyes, cleft chin, and smallpox-mottled face.

"'The Lord doth give, the Lord doth take away. Amen.'" The speaker closed the Bible and stepped to the coffin, removing the lid and placing it on the other two sawhorses. "And now, brethren," he said dolefully, "you can all take your final look, but please hurry it along. I still have to package him for the nine o'clock train."

Everyone stood and began shuffling toward the casket. Bishop eased into line a few mourners in back of the familiar man. Hat in hand, he slowly filed with them to pay his last respects. When it came his turn, he glanced inside, blinked, then made a closer inspection.

The corpse had been fitted with a white shirt, black bow tie, and a threadbare cutaway suit. Black socks were on his shoeless feet. His once strong, capable hands and full-fleshed face were now gaunt and stringy, and his dark-tanned skin had turned to a waxy blue-gray pallor. The mortician, in a fit of inept artistry, had daubed a couple of spots of rouge in the center of the corpse's aged, wasted cheeks.

The effect made Timotheus Tighe look ghastly.

CHAPTER 2

Bishop lurched away from the casket, stunned. He stepped off the podium, still keeping the familiar man in close view, but his mind dwelled on the dead old lawman, lying in state.

There was no sense of happiness, of relief. Instead there was a lump in Bishop's throat, and a tight sadness gripped him, as though Tighe had been a close relative instead of an implacable enemy. In a way, he and Tighe were akin, both having spent hard and lonely lives, mostly in the saddle. The only real difference between them, Bishop supposed, was that they'd lived their lives on opposite sides. Well, the chase was over, and not necessarily won by the better man.

Bishop shook himself free of his melancholy, seeing that the other man was already at the drapes. He quickened his pace, passing through and catching up with the man just outside on the boardwalk.

With the man was the plump lady organist. She was looking sternly at him, as if he were a recalcitrant child. He was looking vaguely off to one side, his features slack with boredom and resignation.

Bishop sauntered up to the man. "Hello, Shelby."

The man jerked, swiveling. "Who? You've got the wrong man."

Bishop grinned. "Don't you remember me?"

"But my name isn't . . ." Shelby faltered, eyes widening, then, "Mygawd, it can't be. It is! Matt, you ol' renegade! Mygawd!"

"Harold," the woman said sharply. "Your language."

"Sorry, m'dear," Shelby replied, turning back to her. "But meet a long-lost friend of mine, Matt Bishop. Matt, this is my wife, Cornelia."

Bishop politely tipped his hat. The woman gave him a once-over as if inspecting a garden pest. He couldn't really blame her for dismissing him as a chuckline tramp; he looked like one, and often had been one. Still, it rankled him, and he gave her the eye right back.

Harold Shelby's wife had a squarish head and gray frizzled ringlets for hair. Her face was etched with lines, especially around her pursed mouth; her figure was shapeless; and her hands were rough and spatulate. She was wearing steel-rimmed spectacles, a baggy floral-print dress, and a pointy-brimmed hat stuck with feathers that was the ugliest hat Bishop had ever seen. All in all, she had less sex appeal than a mud hen, and Bishop decided he did not care for her one whit. He could also sense that the feeling was mutual.

"Matt rode shotgun back when I drove the Butterfield Overland," Shelby hurriedly told his wife, and, before Bishop could deny it, he rushed on. "Those were the times, eh, Matt? Them pesky redskins raring to lift our hair and hide, save for you and your Winchester."

"Oh, yeah, right," Bishop responded, catching on. Obviously Shelby had bragged about being a stagecoach driver, no doubt one of many whoppers he'd spread in order to be accepted in whatever passed for society in these parts. "Those were wild times, okay."

Cornelia tapped her foot. "Staying long, Mr. Bishop?"

Bishop exchanged a swift glance with Shelby. "No longer'n it takes to grab a bite to eat, ma'am. It was just that I happened to be passing through Sugarwood, and thought I'd look up my ol' sidekick."

"Well, the Eats Cafe serves good food. And Shelby has little time for old days now, I'm afraid, our store being *so* demanding," Cornelia told him haughtily. "Harold? Come along, we must be reopening for the evening trade, now that the funeral is over."

"Can't Ozzie spell in at the counter for a while, m'love? I'd like to catch a quick cup of coffee with Matt, if I may."

"Harold, you know Ozgood isn't allowed to do strenuous work."

"Well, if'n you fear our son will wreck his delicate constitution," Shelby drawled slyly, "I guess Matt could come over to the store and stick around for dinner with us. Wouldn't that be nice, m'dear?"

Cornelia stiffened, glaring at her husband, her nostrils dilating. "Don't dawdle over your coffee, Harold. And if Ozgood strains himself, I'll . . ." She ended her threat with a waspish sniff. Then giving Bishop an angry, defiant scowl, she pivoted and flounced off across the street, raising her dress a little to miss the mud.

"You wouldn't have liked to eat at my place anyway, Matt," Shelby said with a sigh. "Cornelia learned all of her cooking from her mother, and her mother was the lousiest cook in Kansas."

Bishop smiled, but thought better than to comment. He watched Shelby's wife unlock and enter the door of a wide-fronted, ramshackle building that sat almost directly opposite the depot. It had a loading platform on one side, barrels of merchandise along its front, and a sign hanging from its boardwalk overhang reading: HUMBOLT'S EMPORIUM.

"That's your name now?" he asked Shelby. "Humbolt?"

"No, Humbolt is the fellow I bought the store from. I didn't see no reason to change it, folks having called it Humbolt's for nigh on a couple of generations. Myself, though, I took the name Loveless when I caught on to the fact that Tighe was investigating every Shelby he could find. Loveless. I never guessed then how right I'd be."

They started up the boardwalk toward the cafe. The storm had tapered to a sullen drizzle now, its front slowly moving southward. And Sugarwood was beginning to revive, the boardwalks filling up and the shops attracting customers, and the drivers of mud-bogged wagons flogging their teams to wrench them unstuck.

"I can't get over it," Shelby said as they walked. "You're a shock for sore eyes, Matt. How'd you track me down?"

"I didn't. I came here on account of Tighe."

"That was fast. He only died day before yesterday."

"Didn't know that, either. Just happened to read about him catching those prisoners, is all." Bishop hesitated, not wishing to explain further; he wasn't sure he could explain his compulsion to himself, much less to Shelby. So he asked, "What'd Tighe die from?"

Shelby didn't reply at once. Then, "My confession."

"How's that? Run that by me again."

"I confessed, Matt. I told him I was Shelby and how I'd been fooling my wife and everybody else here with my phony name and past."

"Why'd you do a goddamn stupid thing like that for?"

"Keep your voice down," Shelby cautioned, wincing as he glanced about. "For the twenty years I've lived here," he continued in a low voice, "nobody's come close to suspecting me, including Tighe. Why, he'd even joke about my first name being the same as an old outlaw he was still hunting and that he'd heard might be in this area. That's why he came here and took the deputy's job. But I finally couldn't bear it any longer, Matt. I couldn't swallow my own lies any longer."

"Weren't you scared?"

"Petrified. But hell, he couldn't have arrested me, only exposed me. To tell the truth, that's what frightened me the most, having my reputation, my position, ruined and my business bankrupted."

"Yeah, that sort of thing always meant a lot to you."

"Well, right up till I told Tighe, I thought it did."

"Doesn't seem your position has suffered, for all your talking."

"That's only because Tighe took my secret to his grave."

"You mean he agreed to keep silent?"

"No, I mean he got so excited that he had a heart attack."

Bishop began to chuckle. "You're kidding."

"The hell I am. He let out a squawk and keeled right over, right there in his office. Died instantly, according to the doc."

The chuckle became a laugh. It was perverse, Bishop knew, but the irony of Tighe having a stroke when finally confronting one of his long-sought robbers was simply too appealing to his sense of humor. And he couldn't stop laughing until they'd reached the cafe.

"I'm sorry," he managed, pausing at the cafe's entrance to wipe the tears from his eyes. "But oh goddamn, that's a choice tickle."

"It was awful," Shelby growled, brushing past and stalking inside. "I can't see anything funny about it at all."

The Eats Cafe was a gloomy room, with hardly more to it than its smattering of tables and chairs. At the rear was a Dutch door, its upper half swung open, revealing a portion of the kitchen on the other side. A Chinese girl about twenty was leaning on its bottom half, arguing in her native tongue with an unseen chef, who liked banging pots and pans. There weren't many customers, this being too early for the dinner crowd, so Bishop and Shelby were able to select a corner table where they wouldn't be easily overheard.

When the girl came over to take their orders, Shelby said to Bishop, "They've a blue-plate special here that'll fill your tapeworm."

"I don't think I can afford that much."

"It's on me, then." Shelby ordered the special for Bishop and two coffees, and when the girl left, he regarded Bishop in mock disgust. "Broke, eh? I might've guessed. But what'd you do with all your money?"

"Don't ask. I don't know," Bishop answered wearily. "It just dribbled through my fingers, and when it was gone, I sort of slumped back into my old habits. I wasn't smart, the way you were."

Shelby shook his head. "My share is just as gone, Matt."

"You bought that store. Hell, you're *making* money."

"Some. But I can't get out what I sunk into my place unless I sell it. And what I didn't invest in it, Cornelia put into the bank. She thinks my loot is from gold panning in Nevada, but never mind. Point being, she considers what's in the store and the bank as her life insurance, and it'd be *my* life to dare try touching any of it."

Shelby lapsed into silence as the girl served the special and coffees, then he asked, "Must you really pull out this evening?"

"Actually, I'm tired and plan to lay over the night at the hotel. Only your wife didn't act like she wanted to hear that."

"Shrewd of you. Where're you figuring to head next?"

"Can't say I've given it much thought." Bishop shrugged self-effacingly, adding, "Can't say I've ever given it much thought."

Shelby contemplated his coffee cup for a long moment. "Think about it tonight," he finally said. "See if you can't think of somewhere half-assed interesting to go. And if you do think of one, Matt, then in the morning before you leave, do me a favor."

"What?"

"Take me with you."

"Why? You've got everything you ever wanted right here."

"Don't rub it in. I know, I'm the guy who always hankered for wealth, influence, for social position. And look what I wound up with: a business that's a twelve-hour-a-day stone around my neck; a dragon of a wife whose only interest in me is my money; two snot-faced daughters who married just as soon as they could get pregnant; and a whiny slob of a son who's still Mommy's angel, and who'll never do an honest lick of work for as long as he breathes."

"Yeah, it is kind of strange how life can trick you."

"Matt, I don't have the guts to do it cold, but I'd leave in a flash if given some excuse. That's why I confessed to Tighe. As much as I feared it, deep down I wanted him to force me out of town."

"Well, drifting with me isn't an answer."

"But it's a hope, don't you see?"

Bishop indeed could see the misery and discontent in Shelby's eyes. Irritated and slightly embarrassed, he turned his attention back to the special, which was a gargantuan steak embedded in a mountain of scalloped potatoes. Yet, as he ate, he couldn't help brooding over Shelby's plight and, for that matter, his own. And by extension, he began to contemplate all that loot, and how it hadn't guaranteed the success of their grandiose plans—the reason for having stolen it.

"I wonder," he mused, chewing thoughtfully. "I wonder if Guffy and Crandon were able to fare any better than we have."

"They must've. Haven't you ever tried to find them?"

"Thought best not to. And it's too late to try now."

"Maybe not." Shelby's pleading eyes took on a fresh glitter, and he leaned across the table. "Ol' Tighe kept a notebook on everything he learned about us. I've got it hidden back in the store."

"How'd you get it? Burgle his office?"

"Of course not," Shelby said indignantly. "Someone had to collect his belongings, so they could be sent with him to his relatives in Ohio. I merely made sure that the someone was me."

"And then you should've chucked it in the nearest fire."

"I planned to. I planned to burn it soon's I was done reading it, but a new notion's just come to me. We'll bring it along instead."

"We? Do what?"

"Tomorrow morning, Matt. You take me with you, and I take the book, and we'll use it to go searching for Guffy and Emmett."

Bishop was genuinely astonished. "You must be drunk."

"I'm as stone sober and serious as I've ever been. But it's like when I had that inspiration for the robbery, Matt, this's just occurred to me in a rush. Tighe's notes can help us find them."

"Fat chance. Tighe didn't do no good with them."

"Tighe didn't know what we know about us. I bet if we put it all together, we can come up with some ideas where to look. Think of it, Matt, us four having ourselves some high old times again."

"Old times, my arse. We'd have nothing but some tired old bones."

"At least let me dig out the notebook and show it to you. Maybe you still won't want to try, but the way I figure, this'll give me my excuse to ride out, and you your someplace to head for." Shelby rose, grinning eagerly, charged with that same enthusiasm which had resulted in the Canta Lupe heist. He tossed a few dollars on the table and gestured impatiently. "C'mon, Matt. You can't tell me you don't have the time. And what else have you got to lose?"

Scowling, Bishop pushed his plate aside and belched politely into his napkin. Slowly, reluctantly, he got up to follow, which was more than he would've sworn he'd have done just minutes before. But Shelby's last argument had him stumped. Shelby was right about him; as usual, he really didn't have anything better to do.

CHAPTER 3

Bishop angled across the street with Shelby, gingerly avoiding the worst of the mud pockets. With evening approaching, the rain had ceased, though there was still a sodden, wintry chill to the air. The saloon was beginning to do a noisy trade, traffic was increasing along the boardwalks, and the wagons were finally finding bottom.

And Bishop was feeling increasingly leery about Shelby's sudden brainstorm. He strongly doubted that Tighe's notebook or anything else could help track down Guffy LeRoy or Emmett Crandon, even assuming they hadn't died or turned senile. And he was far from convinced he wanted to hitch up with them, much less Shelby—promises of high old times notwithstanding. It'd sure put a crimp in his style, or lack of style, he thought. His wandering existence was not the romantic dream he suspected Shelby envisioned it to be. But it was all he knew, and, like most crusty bachelors, he considered himself too set in his ways to be taking on any new partners, male or female. Complications arose when one was in harness, so did obligations.

He had half a mind to sneak away during the night and leave Shelby to his safe but sorry life in Sugarwood. He had also half a mind to let Shelby come along with Tighe's notebook, so he could have a chance to read it thoroughly. There wouldn't be time to do that tonight, he knew, not with Shelby's menace of a wife lurking around; yet he had to admit that he was curious to learn what was recorded about him and wondered if it might stir up a few pleasant memories.

Frankly, he wasn't sure quite what he was going to do. So in his ambivalence, he decided to put off making any decision. . . .

Humbolt's Emporium, Bishop saw when they entered, was a warehouse with farm supplies and household goods stacked and crammed and hanging from the rafters. Near the front door was a long, wide counter with candy jars, a coffee grinder, and a paper-and-string dispenser. Behind it were shelves of airtights, and barrels and large grain sacks of bulk food. The barrels were on one side, and the sacks on the other, of a large walk-in closet whose door was closed and painted with a big red X. And stretched out on top of the grain sacks was a boy, snoring lustily.

The first thing Shelby did was to yank the boy off the sacks.

The boy gave a bleat, more from being startled awake than from fear of Shelby. "Lay off, Pa. You know Ma don't let you hit me."

"And I ain't about to let you sleep on the job, either."

"Aw, I got bored." The boy was in his mid-teens, stood taller than Shelby, and was flabby all over. His hair looked to have been barbered with the aid of a bowl, and his pugnacious nose and vapid eyes were sunk in fat. He had on work boots of an outrageous size, a sleeveless shirt, and outgrown bib overalls, and what bare flesh he had exposed appeared to have the consistency of suet. "Anyway," he muttered sullenly, "what's the difference? Nobody came in."

"You'd never have known if they had," Shelby snapped, then waved his hand dismissively. "Go on, go tell your mother I'm back."

Lethargically, the boy started tramping toward the rear of the store. "Ma!" he shouted, his voice reverberating. "He's here!"

"I'd deny having sired that ox," Shelby growled, "only I can't believe any other man could be desperate enough to bed Cornelia." He glanced despairingly at Bishop. "She was pretty, once. Well, passable. And she was Humbolt's daughter. He lowered the price."

"Ma?" echoed the boy's bull roar. "Pa's here. Can I have something more to eat?" The slam of a door cut off his yelling; evidently the back of the store had been made into the Shelby home.

The instant he heard the door shut, Shelby went to the walk-in closet. "I hid it in here," he said, taking a key from the shelf alongside and unlocking the closet door. "I'll be right out."

Inside the closet were a few used pistols and rifles, and a much larger stock of ready-made ammunition, supplies for loading one's own, and heavy, squat canisters of powder. Shelby slid one of the canisters aside, reached down behind a loose board in the wall, and pulled out a dog-eared, brown leather binder.

"Tighe indexed by name," he said, returning and opening the binder on the counter. "That was his method, to list everyone he could discover who had one of our names, and then check them out."

The pages were yellowed, many of them mere scraps and memos wedged in loose-leaf. Some of the earliest entries had faded almost to obscurity, and the later ones which were still legible were done in a crabbed, spidery scrawl nearly impossible to decipher. Bishop didn't even try to, but asked Shelby, "What's in there about me?"

"Not a lot of different Bishops," Shelby replied after a quick scan. "Mainly it's like a diary of where you'd drifted and left."

"Yeah, he latched onto my back-trail fairly fast."

"Must've driven him frantic, though, to've never quite caught up with you." Shelby thumbed through the binder a bit more. "Look at all these places you were. Why didn't you ever settle down, Matt?"

Bishop shrugged. "Never found the right woman, I guess."

Which was a lie, and he knew it. He had found the right woman, once. A girl, actually, his age—Heloise Flynn. And they'd fooled around together since they'd been pups, until the afternoon he'd ridden over to her father's ranch, the Flying F, and found her and ol' Zeb Flynn and Junius Algernon all dressed up on the porch. And Zeb, wanting the good life for his motherless daughter, had wasted no time in announcing to Bishop that Heloise had just married Junius, son of Ichabod Algernon, the head of Canta Lupe Bank & Trust.

Somehow Bishop had managed to stammer his best wishes to the new couple. Had Heloise shown the slightest regret or sympathy it might have helped salve his wound, but she had been serenely indifferent. Which, in afterthought, Bishop had reflected kinda fit her, because she'd never bothered to drop a word that she'd become engaged. He'd been racked over by a pair of female spurs, alright, and following her, no woman and not much else seemed worth trusting or caring about.

But that was all dead history, the livid scars healed over and the injury forgotten. Irked at having even recalled Heloise at all, Bishop urged grouchily, "Try the Crandons, for Emmett."

"No Emmetts, of course," Shelby said, perusing the list. "I'll look for gamblers. Nope, nothing here about gambling Crandons."

"Emmett wouldn't be a gambler no longer. He was always talking about quitting once he'd raised Big Casino, and then parlaying his stake in the stock market, or in some other sorta speculation."

"No different than dealing cards, you ask me."

"Mayhaps not, but run down that line of Crandons again, and see if there ain't some of them with tycoon-type occupations."

Shelby began a more careful study. "Christ, there're lotsa Crandons," he muttered as he read, "and they're all working at lotsa dumb jobs." Suddenly he stopped, stabbing the paper with his finger. "Here's a pretty new entry I guess Tighe didn't get a chance to follow up on, but listen: 'Crandon, first name unknown, purportedly owner and operator of Casino Petroleum Products, Torment, Oklahoma.'"

"Well, you can't be in a more high-rollin' game than oil, but it's hard to imagine Emmett muckin' about those fields. Any others?"

"Casino," Shelby mused thoughtfully. "I know I heard . . ."

"I just said it," Bishop retorted testily. "Emmett sometimes called his stake that. 'I'm gonna make me Big Casino one of these nights, and take off a-flyin',' he'd say, specially when we were playin' casino, which we did 'pon occasion, remember? And now that you know why it sounds so familiar, forget it and let's get on with it. What else is there in them Crandons that might fit?"

"That's more or less it. LeRoy's got even less."

"Odd. Hell was always poppin' when Guffy was around."

"Well, it shows some dead-end leads, but mostly it's blank."

"I'd have bet that more'n any of us, Guffy would've become a notorious outlaw by now—if not shot first, divin' out a bedroom window."

Shelby glanced up, grinning broadly. "Remember the night afore the robbery? When we was all wound up at the Social Club, and Guffy was upstairs with that one sweetie he had a bad swoon for?"

"Ah . . . Aurora, she called herself. Aurora Borealis."

"Uh-huh, and he was poking her so hard, her bed collapsed?"

Bishop broke out laughing. "And it shook the plaster off the ceiling, down in the barroom where we were waitin'? Oh, goddamn!"

Shelby laughed along with Bishop as he continued flipping through the pages. Then abruptly he sobered up, sucking in his breath, and riffled back through to a previous spot. "No, you're wrong, Matt. I'm wonderin' if you're not wrong."

"The plaster did too come down. I remember it clearly."

"Not that. Crandon. Don't you see?" Shelby said in a hushed voice. "That'd be Emmett, Matt, that'd be what he'd name his company. He was after Big Casino and he won it—Casino Petroleum."

"Harold, if you figure to locate Emmett by what he went

after the most and won, you'd better look for a name like Roundheels or–"

"Ah-hah!" a voice cut in from behind them. Both men spun in startlement, gaping as Shelby's formidable wife bore down on them.

"So Ozgood was right about you," she thundered at Shelby. "He said you were loafing with a hobo, but it's only *him* again."

"Now, dear, I can explain–"

"And striking poor li'le Ozgood, too!" She halted almost toe to toe in front of them, hands on her hips, bosom heaving, and her features congealed with indignation. "Brute! How dare you."

"I never touched the bast–Ozzie. He fell off the sacks–"

"Well, we'll have a few words about this later," she said darkly, then turned on Bishop, who was covertly trying to close the binder behind him on the counter. She cast her frosty gaze over his grubby, disreputable appearance again and shuddered. "And you, Mr. Bishop, didn't you tell me you were leaving immediately after eating?"

"The very plans, ma'am," he assured her, edging away along the counter, dragging the binder with him. "Saying good-bye, is all–"

"What's that?" she barked, and before Bishop could protest she had snatched the binder from around his back and was leafing through it, frowning suspiciously. "Where'd this come from?"

"It's mine," Bishop replied hastily. "It's my notes."

"Of his travels, like a journal," Shelby chimed in, and Bishop could almost hear the sweat in his voice. "Matt was showing it to me, all the places he's visited, all the people he's met."

"All the people seem to have the same name."

"Part of my hobby." Bishop extended his hand. "If you'll just give it back, I won't be bothering you nice folks any longer."

"Not so fast," she snapped, and thrust the binder under her arm. "I smell something decidedly fishy going on here, and I think I'd better keep hold of this awhile until I–"

"Oh, no you're not." And Bishop, a streak of orneriness within him refusing to be buffaloed by this she-blister, abruptly lunged forward and wrenched the binder away from her grasp.

"Lay hands on me, will you!" A huge fist came sailing out at Bishop. He ducked, but not far enough, and Cornelia landed a clout alongside his head. The store exploded. The sawdusty floor jumped up and met his backbone, and he sprawled gasping, hearing through ringing ears as she berated Shelby. "He came at me, you saw him! Why didn't you protect me?"

"But I reckoned–"

"You reckoned what? Don't stand there braying like a jackass!"

Bishop, trying to gather his legs under him, found that somehow he'd managed to retain the binder. Now to get up, get past her, and get out. The only time he'd ever struck a woman, she had been no lady; she'd been the madam of a house in El Paso, who'd pulled a pistol and demanded his wallet. And, he thought as he wobbled upright, as far as he was concerned, this Cornelia woman was right there in the same unladylike corral. He leaned against the counter for support, baring his teeth and snarling, as if daring her to try to stop him.

"Keep him away, Harold! He's attacking again!" Cornelia reared as if preparing to let fly another haymaker, but Bishop's murderous expression and another deep snarl seemed to change her mind. "Hold him, Harold!" she yelped instead, turning and leaping for the walk-in closet. "Don't let the wretched bum escape! I'll get the shotgun in here and then we'll have him cornered!"

"And she'll have the notebook," Bishop hissed.

"Dear sweet Jesus, not that." Fear had frozen Shelby useless, but now pure horror activated him, launching him toward the closet, where his wife was half in, half out, stooping in search of the shotgun. His shoulder rammed the door, jamming it shut on rusty hinges, and propelling her bodily inside. A spiraling scream, and the closet shifted on its foundations as her great bulk met the rear wall, while Shelby rebounded and frantically twisted the key in the lock.

"I'm sorry," he called out. "I'm sorry it came to this."

Shelby's expressions of regret and necessity were lost in the shrill bellows of outrage and the hammering blows of fists and feet. His wife was in no mood for apologies, now or ever.

"Quick," Bishop yelled over the din. "What's the nearest town?"

"Gleneden, about two hours due east, but—"

"Fine. I can hole up there for the night."

"But aren't you going to wait for me tomorrow?"

Bishop stared. "Are you mad?"

"But I'm not ready, I—"

"Then don't come."

"Now who's talking mad?" Shelby glanced at the closet, just as inside a shelf of loading supplies evidently gave way. Its falling clatter produced yet more howls and thumpings against the door, which was beginning to buckle, the wood around its latch already splintering. "Mygawd, and she's getting free," he moaned.

"Goddamnit, grab a coat. And some money, if you can."

"Yeah, yeah." Feverishly, Shelby opened the cash drawer in the counter, cleaning it out, stuffing banknotes and silver into his pockets. Bishop stood by the open front door, gesturing for him to hurry it up. Shelby, nodding, snatched a vintage Iver Johnson .38 from a ledge underneath the drawer and tucked it in his belt, then sprang for a brass coatrack, knocking it over in his haste to grab a worn gabardine overcoat off one of its hooks.

They sprinted up the boardwalk, Bishop clutching the binder to his chest, and Shelby trying to wrestle on his coat as he ran.

"You got a horse?" Bishop asked.

"A mare. She's boarded at the stable."

"Good, so's mine."

"I suppose I have to pay to get yours out of hock?"

Bishop grinned. "How nice of you to offer."

Behind them came the rending of wood and hardware, the shriek of an enraged woman, and the dull volcanic roar of two barrels of 10 gauge number 6 shot erupting in their general direction.

CHAPTER 4

The trail meandered along a low ridge that bordered a small, sluggish river. Bishop reined in along one of the ridge's spines, uncapped an amber-colored bottle he took from his saddlebags, and scowled at Shelby. "You ain't got the sense of direction of a frog," he complained, tilting the bottle. "If you hadn't been so all-fired adamant to take this turn instead of the other at that last fork–"

"We'd have ended back up in Tulsa again," Shelby cut in, the sight of the bottle glued to Bishop's lips adding surliness to his voice. "Or at some faraway ranch or dead-end oil rig. But sure as hell that other turn wouldn't have led us to Torment."

Shelby had his gabardine coat tied to the saddle behind him. And at the first crossroads store they'd passed, he had traded his Sugarwood go-to-meetin' clothes, the ones he'd worn for Tighe's funeral, for a pair of tan twill pants and a fawn-colored shirt. The pants fit too narrow around his paunch, and the shirt was too loose across his shoulders, and the secondhand holster for his Iver Johnson .38 rubbed against his thigh. But the bottle appeared to him to be of perfect size, and he snapped, "Mygawd, save me a nip."

"Don't get yourself in an uproar," Bishop retorted, wiping his mouth and handing across the bottle. He added querulously, "At least at a ranch or an oil rig, we could've asked for directions," and straightened in his stirrups to survey the country around them.

Ahead, the Oklahoma flatlands stretched in hillocks and corrugations toward the Texas border. To the west and north rolled more of the same, but to the east, highlighted by the morning sun, rose the distant foothills of the Jackforth mountain range. The shallow excuse of a river, which they'd been paralleling since the fork, flowed from the foothills northeasterly of them; shading his eyes against the glare, Bishop could just make out the silhouette of a large ranch house nestled among the cottonwoods and diamond willows, where the river and the foothills seemed to meet.

Goddamn Shelby appears to've been right about that fork, Bishop thought grumpily. And, as he moved his gaze southerly along the foothills, he had to admit that Shelby might also be right about this trail heading toward Torment. Because, by squinting, Bishop could vaguely perceive the clustered outlines of some buildings and tents, though their distance was too great to be sure of even that.

However, a mile or so further up the trail could distinctly be seen a wildcatter's tar-paper shanty and the dark spars of his oil rig. Bishop, pointing, said, "We'll stop at that place just yonder."

Shelby lowered the bottle and bit into a chaw of tobacco. "Whatever for, Matt? Torment's only two, three hours more to go."

"Maybe it is, and maybe it's somewhere else. And I'm in no mood to ride all thataway only to find you lost us." Bishop deftly plucked the bottle back and settled in his saddle. "Besides, we can use some food. Some good, hearty, home-fried food."

"Food!" Shelby spat a brown stream over his mare's left ear. "You overgrown tapeworm, you ain't finished picking your teeth from breakfast yet!"

"I can smell the cookin' already," Bishop said, cheerfully ignoring Shelby's outburst, and returning the bottle to his saddlebag, he heeled his chestnut gelding forward in a sprightly trot.

Descending from the ridge, the trail became tacky, almost sticky, from the countless dribbles and spills of passing oil transports and equipment wagons. Many of the paths and roads

Bishop and Shelby had traveled in Oklahoma were this way, especially along the flats and in the depressions where the oil seemed to seep down and coagulate. They were distressing and somehow unnatural to an old cowpuncher like Bishop, as were the numerous skeletal derricks and flaring gas wells which marred the pastoral beauty, and the incessant gunshot popping of cable tool boilers that resonated across the surrounding prairie.

They forded the river, which was black-rimed from crude oil washing down from upstream drilling, and came to a fresh wagon path that cut across the earth and shale to the oil rig. Clods crumbled in from the ruts as they passed through the gate of a crudely built fence that enclosed the property. The boiler beside the rig was subdued to a chuffing hiss, and the walking beam arched motionless. The smell of crude oil drifted on the wind, making Bishop's horse snort and shy.

Bishop pulled his horse up and called, "Hello the house!"

A mongrel hound rose hackling from under the shanty's crawl-space. He barked twice, squatted to scratch an ear, then slunk back under the flooring.

"That's odd," Bishop murmured. "A working rig that ain't, and nobody around to tend it nohow." He was about to hail the house again, when Shelby made a coarse hacking noise, and Bishop turned to him, asking disgustedly, "Now what's the matter? You swallow your chaw?"

Shelby, shaking his head, pointed toward the rig.

Bishop followed the line of the finger, again shading his eyes from the morning sun as he tried to plumb the shadows of the grease-blackened derrick. And there, almost invisible against the casings and other equipment, hung a man from the lowest of the cross-spars, his head canted against the rope around his neck.

"Greatgawdalmightydamnit!" Bishop blurted. Dismounting, he went over to the rig's platform and stared up at the man, who was sandy-haired and in his late twenties, and dressed in standard boomer garb. "Neck's broke," he said. "He didn't suffer much."

"Wonderful. Now let's go and leave him in his peace."

"No horse could've been slapped out from under him, not with the platform 'n' stuff in the way." Bishop unsheathed his knife and began slicing through the rope, where it looped down from the spar and was tied to a support post. "Whoever done it must've been goddamn strong, to've yanked him up hard enough to snap his neck. Either that, or it was broken beforehand and set up to look like a hanging."

"They may've been more'n one whoevers," Shelby said fretfully, reluctantly dismounting and glancing about. "And they may come back."

The body crumpled to the oil-slick platform. Bishop, resheathing his knife, stepped over and stooped, picking up one limp hand. "He's not all the way cold yet. He hasn't been dead very long at all."

Shelby clucked his tongue, doffing as a sign of respect the sweat-stained bowler hat he'd bought as a lark with the rest of his duds. "Ain't legal, Matt, cutting a man down after his hanging."

"Ain't legal the way this one was strung up," Bishop replied coldly. "C'mon, help me lug him into his shack, so the animals and birds can't get at him. Then we'll notify the law in that town up ahead."

"Worser and worser. The law'll think we did the lynching." Shelby clapped his hat back on and gingerly hoisted the man by his legs. He took two steps with Bishop, then, panicked by the sound of horses drumming fast along the road from the direction of town, dropped the legs as if they'd suddenly caught on fire. "What'll we do, Matt?"

"Nothin'. We ain't done nothin' wrong, have we?"

"No, but only we know it," Shelby moaned.

They stood watching as four riders galloped into view. The riders, spotting them, abruptly veered and came spurring into the yard, led by a heavyset man with a stubborn, harsh mouth and furrows in his ruddy cheeks.

"What've we got here, boys," the man said in a bull roar of a voice—and he said it as a statement, not as a question. He dismounted even before he'd reined his horse to a complete stop, his three companions following, grouping around Bishop, Shelby, and the dead man in a tight, challenging circle.

Calmly, Bishop began, "What we've got here is a killing—"

"And the killers," the man interrupted loudly. "Looks like we chanced upon them, boys, caught right in the act."

One of the others asked dubiously, "These two, Jiggs?"

"Has to be," the big man named Jiggs retorted. "There's Sy Lowensburg, there's the rope, and there they are."

"H-hold on," Shelby stammered. "W-we found him hanging, and were only moving him for safekeeping before riding to report it to—"

"To whoever paid you two old cutthroats to do in Lowensburg." Jiggs, flexing his chest muscles, stepped pugnaciously up to Bishop and Shelby, his eyes like slate, without depth or feeling. "Why, I wager you're guilty of the other killings and beatings and burnings that've been going on hereabouts."

"Jiggs, is it?" Bishop asked mildly, toeing the earth.

Jiggs blinked, distracted by the unexpected question.

And Shelby whispered, "Don't, Matt, please," wincing as he remembered how Bishop used to act, and fearing he hadn't changed.

And Jiggs, hastily recovering, snapped, "Yeah, that's m'name, and I'm foreman of the Cache Springs Ranch. What's it to you?"

"Well, Jiggs," Bishop drawled, keeping a placid little smile on his face, "I just wanted to know, because the last time I heard such a passing of sour wind, it was coming out the wrong end of a mule."

And he punched Jiggs flush in the mouth.

A concerted gasp went up from the riders, as their boss staggered backward, tripped, and sat down in a puddle of oil. Jiggs's face turned red from blood gushing from his split lips, and his pants turned black as he lurched, sliding in his attempt to regain his feet. And by the time Jiggs managed to stand again, Bishop had him covered with his Colt, and Shelby had his .38 trained, wavering, on the other three.

"*Now* can we go, Matt?" Shelby pleaded.

But Shelby couldn't level his revolver at all three at the same time, grouped as they were in something of a semicircle. Even as he was addressing Bishop, one of them was able to skitter out of his line of sight and jump him. Shelby stumbled, losing his pistol, his bowler hat tipping down over his eyes as he bumped into Bishop, upsetting Bishop's aim.

Jiggs and his other two men leaped. It degenerated into a first-class tavern brawl, a number of good licks put in before the Cache Springs crewmen engulfed Bishop and Shelby. One rider was knocked skidding back into the same puddle Jiggs had landed in. Another was hit soundly on his chin by a solid fist thrown by Jiggs. Yet another was sent limping when Shelby kicked him in the kneecap.

But finally the four younger, beefier men overwhelmed them. The vengeful Jiggs and his infuriated crew surged in an ever-tightening ring, seizing arms, forcing them down. Bishop tripped over one of the scuffling boots, blinding pain from a rabbit punch seeming to shatter his skull. He was pulled to the ground, glimpsing Shelby also being dragged to his knees. He fought his way to his feet using fists, elbows, teeth, his entire body as a weapon. But it was hopeless, and Bishop found himself pinned, breathless and stunned.

Jiggs confronted him, livid with fury. "Ain't no question about you hombres now! Well, you're going to get what you deserve!" Then turning to one of his crew, he ordered, "Wayne, bring the ropes off our saddles. We're going to hoist these two high, just like they did to Lowensburg."

Bishop and Shelby struggled, but were too weakened and dazed to stop their hands from being tied behind their backs. They were dragged unceremoniously over to the platform, where two other ropes had been tossed over the same strut Lowensburg had been dangling from.

"Chrissakes, who'd have thought," one of the men said to a second, spitting out a tooth as they slipped nooses around Bishop's and Shelby's necks. "And this one's no bigger'n my kid sister."

Jiggs licked his battered lips. "Ready?"

"Not so fast," Shelby yelped, eyeing the crew as they prepared to pull on the ropes. "Maybe Matt here was a mite fractious, but Matt never had no proper upbringing anyway. Neither did I, come to consider. And maybe we look kinda bad to you, the way you come upon us and all. But this ain't right, either, not allowing a fair hearing–"

"Haul on them ropes, boys," Jiggs interrupted, overriding Shelby's pleas with his bellowing voice. "We've given these two all the hearing they'll ever get. Now let's see them do some dancing."

"Don't!"

The loud counter-command sheared through the yard, freezing the crew with their hands on the ropes. A rangy, shaggy-haired man rode his roan up to the platform, the morning sun reflecting off the shiny star fastened to his leather vest. His eyes, gray and piercing, surveyed the scene from under drooping lids, his right hand resting loosely on the butt of a Colt Peacemaker holstered on his hip.

"What's going on here?"

Jiggs grinned wolfishly. "A hanging, MacGrueder."

"Sheriff MacGrueder, to you," the lawman stated. "And I'll thank you not to do my job for me. Now, get those ropes off them."

"You're making a mistake–"

"If anybody's guilty of a hanging offense, they'll get hung. But only after a proper trial. Get those ropes off!"

Sheepishly, the men holding the ropes let go of them and hastened to remove the nooses from Bishop and Shelby. But they made no move to untie the wrists, and Sheriff Mac-

Grueder, evidently wanting it that way, turned his attention to the body of the dead wildcatter.

"This more of your handiwork, Jiggs?"

"That's what I'm trying to tell you," Jiggs answered angrily. "We were riding back to the ranch when we caught these two red-handed."

"You actually saw them string up Lowensburg?"

Jiggs hesitated. "Not exactly. Saw them with the body."

"We found him hanging," Shelby repeated, "and were only moving him for safekeeping before riding to report it to you, Sheriff."

"This ol' muskrat tried feeding me the same windy," Jiggs sneered. "It can't be true, on account Lowensburg was fine when I rode by here earlier this morning, on my way to town. He waved to me, matter of fact. Anyhow, my boys here had been whoop-de-doing it too much and had stayed over the night, which is why I had to go get them. I met them along the way, and we started back, and none of us, either coming or going, saw or heard anybody else the whole time."

Sheriff MacGrueder eyed Bishop and Shelby with deepening suspicion. "Well, we'll just take them in and see what we can see," he said, adding, "Now, there're a couple of pistols lying near your feet, Jiggs. If they're theirs, bring 'em to me. And one of you others, get that noose off Lowensburg and bring him along to town."

Jiggs gestured to his men and started collecting the pistols, while his "volunteers" flipped a coin to see who'd ride double with the corpse. And the sheriff told Bishop and Shelby, "If you can get yourselves seated, you ride. If you can't, you walk."

With their wrists bound, Bishop and Shelby were forced to struggle in ungainly balancing acts in order to gain their saddles. By the time they had, the sheriff had stowed their weapons in one of his saddlebags; and Sy Lowensburg had been stripped of his knife-cut stub of a noose, and had been tossed across the losing man's horse.

"Let's go." Nodding with wary satisfaction, the sheriff took the reins of Bishop's and Shelby's mounts and urged them into a slow canter, riding with his two prisoners flanking him. Jiggs and the man named Wayne fell in behind, and trailing came the other two riders and Lowensburg, with his hands and feet trussed to cinch rings.

CHAPTER 5

The trail unraveled through what had once been pristine rangeland, but which now was infected with splotches of petroleum blight. Large ugly areas were coated with tarry wastes, and Bishop wondered if grass would ever grow again in these ruined patches.

He hadn't spoken much since the brawl with Jiggs and his crew, because he hadn't felt there'd been much worth saying. No words could've altered Jiggs's mind, and his men were obviously under his thumb; and no amount of denials or arguments would've dissuaded Sheriff MacGrueder from doing his job as he saw fit. But mainly Bishop hadn't said his piece because the fight had exhausted him to a frazzle.

After riding awhile, though, and resting despite the hassle of keeping seated with his hands tied behind him, Bishop began feeling chipper enough to ask the sheriff, "Where're we heading? Torment?"

"Yep."

"Does Emmett Crandon live there?"

"Yep." And the sheriff left it at that.

They rode some more in silence, and then Bishop tried a different tack. "Don't this seem mighty coincidental, Sheriff? We happen to stop at Lowensburg's, then this Jiggs fellow and his men come along, then you show up. Or is there something special going on?"

"Well, yes 'n' no, but I'd figure it's mostly accidental. And bad luck for you two. It's pretty common for Jiggs to hafta corral some of his wandering crew and herd them back to Cache Springs Ranch—"

"That the big spread you can see northeasterly of here?"

"That's it. And me— Well, Lowensburg lodged a complaint with me yesterday, about being roughed up to make him sell out his oil lease and rig, so I thought I'd check on how he was doing, while the day was still quiet for me." MacGrueder paused, then added as if irritated at himself, "But I've a hunch I'm repeating what you already know."

Shelby, who'd been overhearing the conversation, piped up, "You've got us wrong, Sheriff. We're strangers from up Kansas way and never been through these parts until today. Only reason we stopped at that wildcatter's was to ask directions to Torment, where we planned to visit our old saddle-pard, Em Crandon. You say you know him?"

Before MacGrueder could respond, Jiggs scoffed, "Them being friends with the likes of Emmett Crandon? It's plain they're liars."

"I see your mouth has been shut once already," MacGrueder said, leaning in his saddle to look back at Jiggs. "Keep it shut."

Jiggs gave the sheriff a sulky glower, but said no more. And because it was apparent that MacGrueder was in no mood for conversation, everyone else lapsed silent for the rest of the trip.

The ride took the better part of two hours, mostly across gently rolling prairie, though the last portion turned more rugged and boulder-strewn with the beginning slopes of the foothills. And the longer they rode, the closer they came to Torment, the more sodden the trail became from oil spillage, occasionally running like a mucky dike between gullies and washes soaked in wastage. From an increasing number of rigs, boilers could be heard roaring, and boomers could be seen climbing about the towers, while other roughnecks worked around the winches and pulley houses. And the terrain grew littered with slush pits, cast-off machinery, and black, wooden tanks, and was crosshatched by valve-studded pipes that were twisted and bent and clustered in angles that defied reason.

Torment was like Sugarwood in that it had only one main street and had a history of being a drowsy whistle-stop for local ranchers and farmers. But there the similarity ended. Now Torment was a boisterous boom town, its street churned to an oily mire by the constant traffic of horses and wagons and even a few of those newfangled gasoline-powered automobiles and trucks.

And as MacGrueder blazed a path down the street, Bishop saw that surrounding the original old false-fronted buildings were solid thickets of fast-sprouting shanties and tents. Some served as supply houses and merchandise marts, but most were saloons, gambling dens, and cribs. Pressing their entrances or milling along the narrow plank walkways were knots of wildcatters, laborers, lease hounds, and speculators. And hanging over everything like a miasma were the dank, cloying smells of crude oil and well gas.

What mainly caught Bishop's eye were two massive structures. The one at the near edge of town was set somewhat apart from the common squeeze and was evidently Torment's answer to a gentleman's drinking establishment; it was festooned with gingerbread, had flaring pole lamps, and two spieling barkers outside to lure customers through its batwings, and in its tall frosted windows was etched the name ROYAL GUSHER. The other, about in the middle of town, was the GRAND NATIONAL HOTEL & RESIDENCE, according to its sign; it had three full stories and cupolas, a half-moon drive curving to its veranda and lobby, and another drive leading to a private stable in back. Both obviously dated initially from Torment's bygone era, and had been expanded and embellished to handle the new, prosperous hordes; and both lorded over the instant hovels clustering near them.

Passing the hotel, MacGrueder reined in beside a low, stone building. "Dismount," he told Bishop and Shelby, and they struggled to get down without twisting an ankle or falling flat on their faces.

Remaining seated, Jiggs watched with a scornful smirk.

"I'll see you again," Bishop said, eyeing him cooly.

"Dangling from a rope, you will," Jiggs retorted.

"That's enough, Jiggs," MacGrueder said. "You men wait here while I lock these two inside. I'm going to need your statements, and we'll have to take Lowensburg here over to the undertaker's."

The sheriff prodded Bishop and Shelby into his office. It and the trio of cells beyond seemed dark after the bright sunlight, but instantly apparent were the noisy flies buzzing at the one grimy glass window, and the strong odor of sweat and urine in the stifling air.

"Mygawd, hang me now," Shelby muttered, gagging.

The sheriff took down a ring of keys and motioned for them to enter the first cell. Then cutting the ropes from around their wrists, he locked the door shut on them and said, "End of the line, fellows."

"It might just goddamn well be, at that," Bishop sighed, sitting down on the iron cot and glancing up at the barred cell window.

The sheriff tossed the keys onto his littered desk, found a piece of scratch paper, and wet the stub of a pencil. "I'll get to your side of the story later, but right now I want your names."

Shelby, clutching the bars, stammered them both out, and Bishop, rising from the bunk, added, "And go tell Em Crandon we're here."

The sheriff, writing laboriously, paused to regard their oil-smeared, battered countenances. "Mr. Crandon is an importance here."

"Well, *this* is important. We know him, I tell you."

"Only he might be too busy to know you."

"Well, move your goddamn butt and find out!"

"Wise ass, eh?" MacGrueder stalked across his office, flinging the paper and pencil onto his desk and selecting a Marlin .38-55 repeater from his gun rack. "Let me hear that again," he bristled, cocking the rifle. "Just let me hear you tell me how to do my job."

"Why, you cowhocked nitwit, I–"

"Shut up, Matt!" Shelby bleated, hastily tugging Bishop back to the cot. "He's sod-headed stubborn enough to pop us a good'n."

After a final warning grunt, MacGrueder, stone-faced, returned his rifle to the rack. Then muttering, "Now for Jiggs and them," he went outside, locking the door of his office behind him.

"Matt, did you have to do it?" Shelby asked disconsolately. "You got Jiggs and his crew so riled that they were going to hang us on gen'ral principles. Now you argufied the sheriff dead against us, and we don't even know for sure if this Crandon fellow is *our* Crandon."

Bishop blew Shelby a raspberry and reached into his shirt pocket for a "short six" cigar. Shelby backed away, shuddering, as Bishop struck a match and lit it. "Mygawd, not another of those!"

"It'll help stifle the stench that's in here already," Bishop replied blandly, but in deference to his cellmate he went to smoke his cheap, pungent cigar by the barred but glassless window.

By craning, he could see some of the street and a small portion of the train yard farther on. Standing there, idly watching and smoking, Bishop brooded about the mess they were in. True, the only evidence against them was the testimony that they'd been standing over the body, that Lowensburg had been alive earlier, and that no one else had been seen on the trail. As ironclad proof, it had more holes in it than a sieve, but logic was secondary here. Jiggs had accused them of other killings and mayhem, and the sheriff had inferred there were claim jumpers operating. So considering how folks get prickly and leap to conclusions about such things–and how Jiggs and crew, well-known and working for a prominent ranch, would influence local judgment far more than two disreputable, alibiless strangers could–for them merely to be found with a murdered man was bad enough for starters.

And quite possibly for enders, too. . . .

The day eased into late afternoon. Although Oklahoma was enjoying balmier weather than Kansas, spring had yet to come, and darkness still came early, bringing with it a crisp, errant breeze.

Bishop continued standing by the window, staring out at the raucous ebb and flow along the street, and across to where, by lamps, the night shift of a section gang was repairing a siding. He fired the last of his cigars and inhaled, his lips pursing, quivering, betraying his frustration and anxiety. . . .

Eventually the front door opened and MacGrueder stepped in, pausing to light a kerosene lantern before ushering in three other men. One was in his early thirties, handsome in a slick-haired, thin-moustached, suave sort of fashion, and Bishop did not know him. Nor did he know the second, who was middle-aged, with scanty gray hair, a round florid face, and a heavy gold watch chain slung across the waistcoat of his brown cashmere suit.

But Bishop identified the third immediately. "Emmett!" he called, and Shelby, beside him, laughed as he too recognized the man.

"By Hades, I didn't believe it when they told me," Emmett Crandon bellowed, brushing past the sheriff and pumping hands through the bars of the cell door. "Welcome, boys, welcome!"

Emmett Crandon was the youngest of the four bank robbers, and although at forty-seven age was beginning to press down on him, no softness or excess weight had yet touched him. He wore plain black, a dark fifty-dollar Stetson, and hand-tooled boots. The effect was an aura of somber, sober force, accentuated by his square Saxon face, only slightly blurred around the edges by the years, and by his clever, sardonic, still-youthful eyes. His grin was wide and hearty—yet, behind that grin, Bishop detected something that had not been there in the old days. There was a sadness: a grim, weary sadness.

"This ain't much of a welcome, Em," Bishop said.

"You two don't deserve no better," Crandon retorted. "But

you caught me in a weak spell, so I've arranged bail for you."

"Fifty thousand," the suave man sniffed.

Shelby boggled. "Fifty grand!"

"Murder rates high," the sheriff said, unlocking the door.

"You're free in Mr. Crandon's custody," the suave man explained as Bishop and Shelby filed wondrously out of the cell. "He's mortgaged his holdings for you, guaranteeing your presence at the inquest day after tomorrow, and at any trial that might be required."

"Now, Otis," Crandon said, embarrassed, "you don't have to—"

"But I do, Em, for your own protection. They must be made to understand that failure to appear or an attempt to leave the area will result in forfeiture of your property. You'll be wiped out."

Bishop glared at the man. "Okay, high-pockets, so you don't approve of what Em's done, and even less of us. Who made you the judge?"

"Button your lip, or I'll jug you for contempt," MacGrueder snapped. "Mr. Gerbil's done you a mighty big favor, allowing Mr. Crandon a kinda gentleman's-agreement loan from his bank."

"Let's not leave these, ah, people with a false impression," the florid man suddenly said, moving to the fore of the disdainful banker, Otis Gerbil. "I am Lorenzo Sedgewick, administrator of the late Angus Donovan's estate for his heirs back in Philadelphia. When I arrived, however, to take charge of his Cache Springs Ranch—"

"Jiggs's spread!" Shelby blurted.

"Jiggs has been the foreman, not owner," the unruffled Lorenzo Sedgewick corrected, continuing, "When I arrived, I was appalled to find Torment to be a lawless Babylon. I instantly set to cleaning it up for decent citizens, by appointing a sheriff and paying his salary from the estate, and by persuading Mr. Crandon and Mr. Gerbil here to join me in an ad hoc town council. As new deputies are hired and other improvements made, the taxpayers will assume their proper obligations and rightful vote. Meanwhile, our authority to detain and judge and, yes, even to set bond, is admittedly de facto and arbitrary, but it is all there is. Do you wish to question it further?"

Sedgewick's little speech came out sounding pompous to Bishop, but he supposed it fit the Easterner. And a prig or not, Sedgewick held the whip. Still, it rankled Bishop, and contrarily he asked, "Yeah. What've you done about Jiggs and his crew?"

"They didn't break no law," the sheriff answered.

"They tried to break our necks!"

"No harm done. They just got overheated, is all."

"Which is why," Sedgewick said, "I have fired Jiggs."

The sheriff frowned. "Jiggs is a top hand."

"Jiggs is a top hand with a rope and a saddle," Sedgewick replied, "but he knows nothing about oil and refuses to learn. And I will not allow him or any of my other men to bully, no matter what the provocation, not so long as they work for me."

Sheriff MacGrueder turned and scowled at Bishop and Shelby, as if blaming them for Jiggs losing his job. "Alright, you git."

"We want our weapons first," Bishop said.

"You *what?* You've been held on suspicion of murder, and—

"For hanging a man, not plugging him," Crandon cut in with a smile. "You might as well send them out there starkers, they'll feel so naked without their hardware. And I'll take full responsibility."

Grudgingly the sheriff stomped out of his office to his horse, the others trooping behind. Retrieving the two pistols from his saddlebag and handing them over, he fastened Bishop and Shelby with a steely eye and growled, "I don't know why Mr. Crandon figures you're more'n piss-pot poor, but he does. So I'm warning you, cross him up or get into any more sort of trouble, and I'll drag your mangy old carcasses back into that cell so fast it'll make your heads swim."

Shelby glanced at Crandon and then at Bishop, a bit of feistiness returning to his features. "Reckon you can ask Emmett if we don't stay out of trouble," he said, and tilted his derby rakishly. "The only thing is, we don't care much to be troubled, neither."

"It's God's honest truth, we're peaceable men," Bishop added, chuckling. "And right now, I'm a goddamn hungry peaceable man."

Crandon broke out laughing. "You lanky cross twixt a coyote and a feedbag, you ain't changed a hair. That's all you ever could think about, that bottomless pit of a stomach of yours."

"What else is there?" Bishop responded blithely. "C'mon, Em, before your friends here change their minds and chuck us into the calaboose again. And just to go to show you how grateful we are, we'll let you treat us to whatever's the finest feast in Torment."

CHAPTER 6

"When Sheriff MacGrueder asked me about you, I nearly shat a blue flame," Crandon said as they walked up the street from the jail. "You didn't really string up that wildcatter, did you?"

"Of course not," Shelby replied archly, and he launched into an account of the hows and whys—such a detailed story too much for Bishop, who was still smarting from the indignities they'd suffered.

"You two sure beat all," Crandon said when Shelby finished. "But Tighe dying like he did, that's a pip. Hate to hear of any good man going, but t'other hand, can't shed many tears over him. Tighe was one cussed bulldog when he got a hold of something, he was."

"Mixed blessings is how I reckon it," Shelby said.

"Let's toast him over dinner," Bishop suggested hopefully. "We'll give him a right-nice send-off just before the dessert course."

"Won't be long now, Matt. We're almost to the Gusher."

"Whups! I want to chew my food, not drink it."

"The Gusher serves the best chow in town, bar none. Hell, it is *the* place in town, period, take my word for it."

He could readily believe it, Bishop thought, surveying the street with growing aversion. Lining both sides were slapdash eateries, wenching tents, and mostly blind-pig saloons, from whose noxious innards roiled shouting, laughter, and the reek of stale beer and rotgut whiskey. While outside, barkers and shills were yelling inducements to the swarms of boomers and laborers who had finished work and were beginning their night's hellbenders.

"God, give me space tween me and the next fellow," Bishop groused as the crowds pushed and jostled them. "And give it to me without all this damn stink and muck."

"What, you mind this?" Crandon asked in mock astonishment. "Why, this's merely the wisp of the evening, Matt. By ten o'clock, there'll be two dozen fistfights and half as many stabbings."

"I don't know how you can take such hurrawin', Em. But I suppose you must find something worthwhile in it, seeing as how you've made enough money here to be able to cough up our bail."

Crandon shook his head, sighing. "Unfortunately, Matt, it's most all on paper. Securities, leases, receivables, things like that, and Gerbil has them sewn up tighter'n a Christmas goose."

"Damn fool," Shelby said over the noise. "Not that we're going to welsh on you, but you shouldn't have put yourself in hock."

"If you feel that bad about it," Crandon replied, reaching the Gusher's gaudy front, "you can go back and turn yourselves in."

"We couldn't now if we wanted to," Bishop yelled, the mob sweeping them into the saloon like chips down a millrace.

The interior was huge, lit by rows of wagon-wheel chandeliers, and rank with the odors of smoke, liquor, and unwashed bodies. At the far end was a stage, on which a trio of violinists was accompanying a singer; both the fiddling and the warbling were lost in the clamor of the throng. Between the stage and the entrance were tables and chairs packed with customers, a bevy of bare-shouldered girls cajoling them to buy drinks, and a scattering of hard-faced, thick-muscled bouncers to see that business didn't get entirely out of hand.

Above the stage ran a gallery and what appeared to be private quarters, with a staircase leading down to a landing against the right wall. From the landing forward stretched an ornate mahogany bar, behind which six bartenders scuttled, ladling booze with heavy hands. Along the left wall were poker tables, dice games, and the chuck-a-luck and faro layouts where, Bishop was willing to bet, many a small fortune had traded owners.

About midway, however, the left wall had an archway with French double doors. It was through there, Crandon explained, that they'd find the Gusher's dining room. The promise of food propelled Bishop forward, and he was almost halfway to the doors before he noticed what—or rather, who—was directly across from them behind the bar.

It was a grotesquely fat man. He was lounging with his huge bulk pressed against the counter, lethargically smoking a black torpedo cigar, and wearing a colorful plaid vest that made him appear even grosser than he was. The only thing quick about him seemed to be his eyes, which darted back and forth as they checked the teeming scene. They passed over Bishop without hesitation, but, spotting Emmett Crandon approaching, they flashed in recognition.

Crandon returned the acknowledgment with a slight nod, then continued with Bishop and Shelby to plow through to the dining room.

They were veering toward the doors, when out of the crowd, Jiggs came swaggering. "I'll be damned," he jeered loudly. "If it ain't them two who lynched Lowensburg, strutting around free as jaybirdies. . . ."

The three halted a few feet from him. Bishop bit his tongue and said nothing. Nor did Shelby, though he worriedly pursed his lips, and Crandon flexed his shoulders in uncomfortable readiness.

". . . and got me fired," Jiggs kept on baiting, "and horn-swoggled themselves outa jail. Ain't that it? Ain't that what you two did?"

Others, overhearing Jiggs, were watching now, sensing the brewing confrontation. Still Bishop said nothing. Shelby's face tightened. Crandon, frowning, warned, "They're with me, Jiggs. Keep aside."

Jiggs laughed, but there was nothing merry in his eyes. "Hiding behind powerful skirts won't save you. Oughta be an example made of lobos like you, I figure. I'll be double-damned, I will."

Now Bishop said, "You likely will be," with a disarming grin, and he took a step closer. Shelby tried to place a restraining hand on his arm, but Bishop shrugged it off, continuing pleasantly, "Your mouth flapped you into trouble this morning, Jiggs, and now your snoot is trying to stick into more of it."

And he punched Jiggs square in the nose, while with his left hand he gathered Jiggs's shirt front and held the man steady for a second swift poke to the flattened nose, crushing the bones. Then pivoting, he used both hands to thrust Jiggs away from him.

Jiggs went spinning backward, careening into the footlamps of the stage and sprawling on the floor. Snarling curses, he dipped his hand for his holstered revolver. Bishop, having anticipated such a move, was already leaping forward, and booted Jiggs's wrist just as the revolver barked spitefully. Jiggs howled and a panel of the back-bar mirror shattered, and the singer on stage broke off her song and ducked as the revolver sailed past her open mouth.

The bouncers were moving in to corral the ruckus, when the fat man bellowed, "Let 'em be!"

Jiggs remained panting on the floor, blood gushing from both mashed nostrils, but the fight was not out of him by any means. Bishop waited while the bouncers went to work widening the circle. He glanced at Crandon, who was watching off to one side, his face shrouded in concern; at Crandon's elbow stood Shelby, eyes wincing heavenward in prayerful regard. And Bishop kept on grinning his little grin, amused now by the thought that the fat man was inviting him and Jiggs to put on a good show, despite the potential damages to what was evidently the fat man's own establishment.

Suddenly, Jiggs catapulted up off the floor, blood staining his face and shirt. Head tucked and fists swinging, he rushed to grapple Bishop and maul him senseless. Bishop sidestepped and smashed an uppercut to Jiggs's chest, but he couldn't avoid the windmilling blows, and one caught him high on the cheek, closing his eye and slamming him over some nearby chairs and a table.

Jiggs followed with another beefy fist, just as Bishop started rolling off the table. Missing, Jiggs crunched his knuckles into the wood where Bishop's head had been. Bishop, after dropping to a wobbly crouch, straightened and was almost flattened by a chair Jiggs had snatched up to bat him with. He backpedaled and Jiggs pursued, gripping the chair by its back and whirling it high. The chair looped down, sideswiping Bishop, a rung catching his shoulder and a leg stabbing his solar plexus, knocking him almost breathless.

The chair hit the floor and fractured apart, but Jiggs kept right on going, stumbling a little from the force he'd exerted. Bishop clasped his hands together, and as Jiggs lunged past off balance, he slashed downward with a straight-armed, double-fisted hammer blow, striking Jiggs on the nape of the neck. Jiggs collapsed across the pieces of broken chair as if he'd been axed.

Wheezing, Bishop left Jiggs on the floor and went over to Shelby and Crandon. "Experience," he said more cheerily than he felt. "That's the problem with young bucks. When Jiggs gets some more training, though, he might become a fair-to-middlin' scrapper."

"Oh sure," Crandon said, not taken in at all. "C'mon, you rawhided war-horse, let's get to my rooms so's you can clean up."

Bishop looked at Crandon as if he'd been insulted. "I ain't et yet," though he allowed, "Guess I could use a wet towel, maybe."

"Yeah, you're bleeding from your mouth like a stuck pig. And if you can see anything outa your left eye, I'll put in with you."

Bishop persevered, ending up using a napkin in the dining room. The room was a third the size of the saloon, but much more high-class, so it wasn't so crowded that they couldn't get a table. Their table sported real silverware and linen tablecloth and napkins, all with the scrolled crest RG emblazoned on them; and their monkey-suited waiter blanched some when he saw Bishop rinsing his napkin in the finger bowl and plastering it to his fist-pulped lips.

The meal was prodigious, as good as Crandon had bragged, with soup and meat and vegetables and potatoes and biscuits swimming in rich milk gravy. It was eaten with gusto, three rounds of beers, and a great deal of catching up on the last twenty-five years.

After a toast to Tighe and a dessert of Boston cream pie, Crandon asked, "Well, are you two planning to stick around awhile?"

"Can't speak for Harold," Bishop said, "but Torment doesn't cater much to my taste. I'll be moving on soon as we're cleared."

Crandon nodded. "You'll be exonerated at the inquest, I'm sure."

"We were hoping you might like to come with us," Shelby said, "and maybe try to find Guffy and have ourselves a bang-up reunion."

"Tempting . . ." Crandon mused, as if half considering it. "He'd be harder for us to find than I was for you, wouldn't he?"

Shelby sighed. "There's not much in Tighe's book on him, no."

"We'd probably have to go back to where we left Guffy off," Bishop said. "Y'know, on account of the bullet he got in the leg during the robbery, when we had to bribe that crooked vet to doctor him in—what was that place?—Nasty Whore Flats?"

"Naughty Girl Valley," Shelby corrected.

"Wherever it was. Changed its name by now, anyway, I bet. We'd have to try to pick up his trail after he healed and left it. Besides, Em, I can't say finding you has been easy on us at all."

"I know, but Torment isn't all bad. It has its qualities."

"It has?"

"If you're a hustler. Why, the prospects were unlimited when I came here ten years ago, and there's still plenty of oil out there to be had. They're locating new wells every day, it seems."

"And hanging innocent strangers from them while they're at it."

"Folks hereabouts are a bit touchy, I'll grant you that. But don't forget, Matt, it was an innocent wildcatter who was actually strung up. Lowensburg wasn't the first, and he won't be the last."

"Then I'm right, Em. The sheriff let mention that Lowensburg had been threatened, and I got the feeling he was hinting at claim jumpers."

"Claim jumping refers to mining, Matt, not oil. On second thought, it doesn't fit poorly. Whatever you want to call it, there's been a gang operating recently, trying to take over the leases and property of the smaller independents and wildcatters."

"Well, killing the owners doesn't get them to sell out."

"Lowensburg was a talker, either talking against giving in to this gang, or for bringing in troopers to wipe them out. I'd guess he was killed to shut him up and as a warning to others, more than anything. There've been other strange deaths and disappearances, but mostly it's been threats and beatings and fires. Fires are the horror around here."

"Hard to believe such crude, old-fashioned techniques could still work," Shelby said glumly. "It's 1912, after all, the twentieth century!"

"Oh, the gang's been sneakier and more sophisticated than that," Crandon responded. "Through contacts and middlemen, it's been able to give out false reports on oil deposits, and through price rigging and stock manipulation, undercut the price of crude oil, until it becomes impossible for the owners of the wells it wants to compete."

"Has it had much success?"

Crandon nodded. "Some got cold feet and sold out for pennies on the dollar. Others went belly-up and had their leases and holdings auctioned off, for pennies on the dollar. The rest ride light, with rifles always within reach."

"And nobody can prove anything? Nobody can get at whoever's leading this gang? He can't be that big of a man, Em. Who is he?"

"Ah, if we only knew, Matt. If we only knew . . ."

Crandon paused, Bishop and Shelby turning to see why. Through the doors, in a swirl of tobacco haze drifting in from the saloon, the fat man came toward them, his rolling gait slow yet self-assured, and remarkably agile and poised, considering his girth.

"Your drinks are on the house," he said when he reached their table. "Accept it by way of apology for Jiggs's behavior."

"Thanks, Whale," Crandon said, "but it's not your fault."

"I realize it stemmed from the tragic events this morning, Em. But it's my responsibility in that Jiggs is now one of my bouncers."

Shelby barked a laugh. "The perfect spot for his talents."

"Well, Jiggs has been one of my toughest customers, so I figured if my bouncers can't beat him, then let him join them. A temporary job, I suspect. Jiggs is an outdoorsman at heart, and Sedgewick is liable to reconsider when he finds nobody can boss his crew as well. But meantime, I'd hate for any, ah, personal animosities to force the sheriff into rescinding anyone's bail. If I may offer a suggestion, take the rear exit from the dining room when you leave."

"We'll keep it in mind, Whale," Crandon said, and before Bishop or Shelby could interject a stronger opinion, he added, "At times I think you know the news before it happens. Got to admit, Whale, you sure keep your thumb on the pulse around here."

"Have to," the fat man replied smugly. "It's my business to; it's how I got where I am, and how I stay there."

"So what've you heard about Lowensburg's death? I mean, besides the crap Jiggs's been spreading about my friends here."

"Only that it's the work of this ring that's running loose."

"Any fresh ideas about who's the brains behind it?"

The fat man shook his head. "If I knew that, Em, I'd likely wind up dead as Lowensburg. I'll hazard this much, though: at the rate he's going, whoever it is will someday control this quarter of Oklahoma. He'll have the money and power and the politicos to do it."

"If he lives that long," Bishop growled.

"In a fight of this kind," the fat man advised somberly, "it isn't the man who's fastest or strongest, it's the man who looks through the back of his head who survives."

"We'll watch behind us, Whale," Crandon said.

"Do, Em. I'd hate to lose a fine customer like you." Then with a brief, departing smile the fat man waddled away.

Bishop stared at his back. "Whale sure fits him."

"His full name's Whaleson," Crandon said. "He's a shrewd devil, and he knows plenty of people and plenty of what they're up to. Unfortunately, that doesn't make him privy to the goings-on in Tulsa or Oklahoma City, where the gang does its dirty business dealings."

"Your banker should have some sources there," Bishop suggested. "And he'd also be able to help find out who's doing all the buying."

"Don't think we haven't tried that angle, Matt. But it's a circus out there, everyone speculating and negotiating with everyone else, some of it shady, and most of it not involving the gang at all. Why, if I can name one, I can name thirty heavy plungers who've been scratching and scrambling whenever a wildcatter folds, including me, Otis Gerbil, and even Lorenzo Sedgewick."

"The rancher?"

"The administrator of an estate that happened to be a ranch," Crandon reminded Bishop. "And before you think it, let me say it: Sedgewick has the brains and the position and undoubtedly the connections upstate; and it's also true that his arrival came about the same time as the gang started muscling in. But he just looks down that nose of his and denies he's the head or any part of any gang, and swears he's only a sharp trader taking advantage of good deals."

"Have you tried pinning him down more'n that?"

"Might as well pin down a greased rattler. Honestly, though, he's merely saying what the rest all say, and the same sort of suspicions can be leveled against most all of us, too. What it boils down to, is that there's nothing in particular linking him any more'n there is anyone else. The gang doesn't have its name on any office door, after all; it works through dummy accounts and shyster lawyers."

"Very smart," Bishop murmured.

"There's big money here," Crandon said with a sigh. "Big money draws smart men—smart men who're willing to scheme and lie and go to just about any extreme to get at that big money."

Bishop gazed steadily at Crandon as he finished his glass of beer. He didn't say anything, but it was in his eyes, in the wry smile he gave his old bank-heisting compadre. He was asking, *And just how far have you been willing to go, Emmett?*

When they left the dining room, nobody had to say a word, because nobody had any intention of retiring by way of a rear exit. They entered the saloon, where Whaleson was back in his same position behind the bar. He smiled, nodding in a vague sort of approval.

The three started wedging through the crowd and were almost to the entrance when a patron behind them yelled a warning. They turned to see Jiggs bulling toward them, his eyes murderous, his broken nose bandaged with plaster tape across his face to hold it steady.

Bishop had no time to set himself, and couldn't avoid Jiggs as the man tackled him, hitting him in the belly and ribs, shoving him backward toward one of the tall, frosted glass windows. Both men crashed through, landing on the boardwalk outside, sending one of the Gusher barkers pitching aside as they rolled tangled together.

Jiggs had Bishop in a bear hug and was trying for a headlock or perhaps just to throttle him. Bishop kneed Jiggs in the groin, an awkward dig causing little harm but allowing Bishop to wrestle free. He scrambled upright, feeling the cuts on his hands and face from the slivered window glass. Jiggs rose and caromed against the same barker, who was trying to crawl out of the way, nearly tumbling over the barker as the barker went reeling again.

Customers came surging out of the saloon, and more spectators began gathering from along the street, tightening the circle. Whaleson lumbered outside and ballooned his way closer, just as Jiggs sprang at Bishop again. "Back!" Whaleson roared at the crowd. "Get back, give 'em room, lots of room!"

Bishop caught Jiggs around the neck and hung on, enduring Jiggs's hard punches tearing into his body. He repeatedly punched back, a post of the porch overhang behind him making it impossible for him to retreat. Ducking and skipping, trying to evade the savage blows, he managed to maneuver Jiggs around until it was Jiggs who had his back to the post. Then Bishop feinted one to the belly, and when Jiggs dropped his guard, he moved in very close, grabbed Jiggs by the hair with both hands, and pounded his head against the post.

Jiggs heaved and shook in his effort to break loose, but in the process he got his neck twisted askew enough so that he was facing the post, and Bishop was able to batter his nose against the unyielding wood. Jiggs screamed bloody hell and clawed for an escape, but Bishop kept on banging that nose over and over.

Finally Jiggs boxed one of Bishop's ears to ringing, and, insane with pain, he was able to lurch from the post as Bishop's grip slackened. He struck the porch railing instead, belt-buckle high, and he, with Bishop still clinging, toppled in a blundering somersault over the railing and porch deck, into the street.

They both struggled to kneeling positions, but that was as far as either could get. Bishop concentrated on that nose, his fists beating a tattoo against the blood-smeary, useless bandage. Jiggs swung at anything within range, but his blows grew increasingly feebler, his nose the weak spot that was draining him of strength and resistance. Bishop pasted him three more times in the same spot, and he sank down soundlessly in the bed of the oil-brackish street.

Bishop stayed kneeling for a long moment. Then, slowly rising, he groped to the porch post for support, gasping for breath, and he grinned at Shelby, who stood close by, fanning himself with his derby.

He looked at Crandon next. "Okay," he said in a slur, spitting blood from a fresh cut in his cheek, "Now I'm ready for a cleanup."

"What for? Why, I've seen better tussles between schoolgirls in their pinafores," Crandon retorted genially, and, winking, he turned to Whaleson. "What'd you think of it as a scrap, Whale?"

Whaleson was surveying the cracked railing that tilted outward like the break in a bone, and the empty window frame where once had been an expensive sheet of glass, and he was not really listening to what Crandon was asking. "And by an ol' duffer," he was muttering to himself. "The bastard's past the age of settin' in a rocking chair, and just see what he's done, what he's cost me. . . ."

CHAPTER 7

As they started back up the street from The Royal Gusher, Crandon said, "You're both staying with me at the Grand National."

"Thanks, Em, but it's too rich for our blood."

"You're right, but it won't do you no good to balk, Harold. I already arranged while you were in the jug to have your horses stabled at the hotel's livery and your bags brought in."

Which was just fine by Bishop. His entire body ached, blood dripped from his scraggly moustache, and his clothes were stained and smelly from the tar and creosote of the street bed. He gritted his teeth against the sharp throbs of pain whenever one of the throngs around them would jostle or bump into him. But he found refreshing the coolish night breeze, as it rippled the flaps of the noisome tents and carried the shouts and curses above the pitch of the barkers.

When they were nearing the hotel, they were passed by a ponderous, high-carriaged, four-passenger automobile chugging down the street, wedging through the tide of traffic like a steamship through ocean waves. Sitting at the driver's wheel was a white-smocked, goggle-eyed chauffeur; starchly upright in the rear seat was Lorenzo Sedgewick, looking straight ahead.

"Might've known a stuffed-shirt dude like him would ride around in a contraption like that," Bishop muttered, "that's always belchin' and fartin' and stinkin' up God's green earth."

"Sounds more like your horse to me, Matt," Shelby said.

"Can't stop progress," Crandon said expansively. "Fuel power is taking over hay power, Matt, 'cause it gets the job done better and faster. Why, that there is the famous Locomobile Forty, and it—"

"Forty what?"

"I don't know what forty, just forty, is all. Last year, the exact same model of Locomobile won the Vanderbilt Cup race, and it's rumored this'n set back Sedgewick over forty-five hundred dollars."

"Loco, alright," Bishop growled, glowering after the car.

When they reached the horseshoe drive and were walking up to the hotel lobby, they saw Sheriff MacGrueder chatting on the veranda with a salesman-type in a wide-checked suit. MacGrueder, glimpsing them, patted the man on the shoulder in a gesture of good-bye, and the man sidled back into the hotel. MacGrueder remained standing where he was, and when Bishop started up the broad steps, the sheriff told him severely, "So you're already brawling in the streets."

"Next time I'll try to keep it inside."

"There better not be a next time."

"Listen, I didn't start it."

"But you sure enjoyed it, didn't you?"

"Same as you do, MacGrueder, acting like the law."

"*Sheriff* MacGrueder, damn you. I *am* the law, all the law Torment has right now, and if you don't believe me, just go on pushing your luck. You'll find out my badge has teeth in it."

Stiff-legged, MacGrueder stalked down the steps and along the drive. And Bishop, watching him, said to the others, "I wonder if he ain't more dangerous than Jiggs. With Jiggs you know where you stand."

"MacGrueder's hard, Matt, but he's fair."

"Maybe, Em, only never forget he ain't the people's sheriff," Bishop reminded Crandon, as they crossed the veranda and entered the hotel. "MacGrueder is Sedgewick's handpicked, paid-for office boy."

The lobby was the size of a ballroom, plush-carpeted and crystal-chandeliered, and furnished with overstuffed velveteen sofas and overgrown potted palms, all denoting a genteel opulence far removed from the rest of Torment. Crandon paused at the front desk for messages, then led the way up a wide, curved staircase to the second floor and headed along a series of gaslit corridors to the rear of the building.

"I keep a suite here, in back where it's quieter," he explained, unlocking the door and ushering Bishop and Shelby inside.

Like the corridor, the suite's parlor was gaslit; and like the lobby, it had rich, wine-colored Brussels carpets. The mahogany walls were hung with paintings depicting life on the plains—buffalo hunts, Indians in war paint, trappers and army forts—done with more romance than talent. Leathered rockers were set around, flanked by tables and brass spittoons. At the near end were a high curtain desk and a steel safe; along the far wall was a row of three closed doors.

Gesturing for Bishop to follow, Crandon went to the last of the three inner doors. It opened into what was obviously a bedroom, with a brass bed, wardrobe, bureau, and chairs, and two valanced windows in the corner that overlooked the drive and quadrangle of the hotel stable.

"Water was fresh this morning, Matt," he said, indicating the basin, pitcher, and towels on a sideboard. "Then we'll take a look through my closet. I think I've got some clothes that'll fit you."

Bishop began stripping off his filthy shirt. "Thanks, Em."

"De nada." Leaving the door ajar, Crandon returned to the parlor, where Shelby had already made himself comfortable in one of the rockers.

"You've done yourself right handsome," Shelby remarked.

"Well, you ought've seen the house I had outside of town," Crandon replied, offering a box of ready-made Fatima cigarettes. "But I couldn't bear living there after Victoria passed away, so I sold it and moved here. Besides, being in town is better for business."

Shelby puffed once on the Fatima, grimaced, and stubbed it out. "Speaking of your business, Em, I've a hunch there may be more to worry about along that line than about what Jiggs or the sheriff might do."

"If you're meaning what this here gang might do, don't worry. Casino Petroleum is too big, too diversified, to be forced out."

"But you could be bought out. If something happened to us—something that made us very suddenly and conveniently disappear—the bank would have to sell your business at a fraction of its value."

"I could be wiped out tomorrow and not lose a wink of sleep," Crandon said wearily, sinking into the rocker next to Shelby. "Oh, once it meant plenty to me, at the start when it was a challenge to build it up for me and Victoria. Since she's been gone, though, I've kinda lost heart in the daily drudgery of keeping it going. Me and her, we didn't have any kids, and I don't have any other heirs, so sooner or later my holdings will be disposed of anyway. Only thing I'm sorry about is I see now how maybe I've endangered you two."

"Still, you shouldn't have gambled your entire stake, Em," Bishop called while washing in the bedroom. "We'd hate to see you lose your Casino, your Big Casino, now that you've finally made it."

"Oh, I only put up my own personal property."

Bishop poked his head out the door. "Casino isn't yours?"

"Sure, it is. It's just that it's not so . . . private, is all. Y'see, I began like most wildcatters, with a questionable lease and a lot of dumb hope, but when I was lucky enough to make a strike, I learned I was at the mercy of the distributors. So I set up my own marketing company—Casino—and to add more profit and clout I asked some of the other wildcatters to pool their oil with me. From there I began providing a certain amount of backing for newcomers, assuming I figured the potential was there. Often as not, I've been right."

"I see," Shelby said, leaning back in his rocker. "Once they start pumping oil, you're in a position to take them over."

Crandon shook his head. "No, Casino is paid a percentage of

their profits, like a royalty or a handling fee. Actually, Casino is more like a cooperative, because we all help plan where to reinvest in other leases and speculations. In other words, I don't care what is written on the ownership papers, Casino has grown to involve so many people that I feel I've only a share in deciding what it does."

"Good for Casino, Em, but doesn't that hog-tie you?"

"Sometimes, but not as much as if I tried running everything outright. The days of land barons are over, Harold; it's become too complicated, too expensive, and over-expansion will eat you alive before you know it. Unless you're a Rockefeller or a Carnegie."

"Or a Sedgewick?" Bishop asked, toweling himself dry. "You said he was buying like crazy, but I can't see him cooperating with anyone."

Crandon laughed. "You've got Sedgewick pegged, Matt, but he's an angel compared to Angus Donovan. His ranch sits over one of the largest deposits around, but Donovan hated oilmen even more'n he did nesters a half-century ago. Anyhow, when Donovan died, Sedgewick arrived and soon realized that oil would earn tons more'n cattle ever could. He didn't have to worry about development capital, not with what Donovan had squirreled away and what the already rich heirs up in Philly could cough up. But scuttlebutt now is that he's stretched himself too thin. His problem is greed: the field extends past the Cache Springs line, and he's determined to control it all, even what little a neighboring wildcatter might pump through slant drilling."

Bishop put down his towel. "So he's land grabbing?"

"Land grabbing's a mite harsh term, Matt. It's too hard to tell who's doing legitimate business, and who's out to bust heads together. All I can give is my opinion, which is that Sedgewick is getting into trouble 'cause he's too selfish and can't read the writing on the wall."

"Or maybe he's trying to get out of it, but doing some writing of his own," Bishop added grimly, turning bare-chested from the basin to where the porter had laid his war bag. It carried a clean shirt, he remembered, and he preferred wearing his over accepting Crandon's kind offer of clothing. He was beholden enough to his friend, he felt.

The war bag had been placed on the floor between the bureau and one of the windows. Above it on the wall hung a large oval-framed photograph of a woman, and, while tucking in his fresh shirt, he studied the picture. The sepia portrait showed a frail beauty whose features were cut with the exquisite care of a cameo.

"This photo in here," he called, "is it of your wife, Em?"

"Yes. I've one in each bedroom. Victoria died six years—"

"Shh!" Bishop suddenly warned, moving to the window.

Shelby appeared at the door. "What's wrong, Matt?"

"I think I hear company down below us."

Shelby crossed to the other window and glanced out. "Yeah, there's somebody down there. Probably he's just taking a leak."

At first Bishop couldn't see anything. Then, peering, he glimpsed a dark shift of movement and the spark of moonlight reflecting off metal. "Not unless the guy's pissing out of a large can."

Crandon, at the doorway, asked: "A can?"

"Like the kind coal oil is carried in."

Apprehension stiffened Crandon. "The Grand National's kept up, but it's old. It'd go up like gunpowder if it ever caught fire."

"Goddamn!" The three raced out of the bedroom, through the parlor, and into the hotel corridor. "Down here!" Crandon yelled, throwing open a nearby door. "The stairs lead to a rear exit!"

They plunged down the steps two at a time. Even before they reached the bottom landing, they could smell a strong odor of kerosene, and see a puddle where some of it had seeped under the doorsill.

Bishop, who happened to be first, wrenched open the exit door and paused an instant for the others. His hesitation saved his life. Two shots lanced out of the darkness by the corner of the driveway, lead splintering the wood of the doorsill next to his head. He flattened to the wall, drawing his revolver, his moves pure reflex—the acts of a man experienced in self-preservation.

But then, hearing a furtive motion as though the shooter was turning to run, he ducked out in a sprint, chin low and revolver high. Other than a white smear across his face, the fleeing man was hard to target in the gloom. Bishop fired, missed, and the man took to weaving to spoil his aim further, making the end of the drive and veering down the street, to vanish in the swirling crowds.

Cursing, Bishop reholstered his revolver and turned back.

"Tried to burn us out, alright," Crandon growled, kicking a kerosene-soaked bundle of sticks and rags away from the building. "Too bad you didn't pepper that bastard plumb full of holes, Matt."

"Yeah, but I recognized him, Em. It was Jiggs."

"You sure?" Shelby asked. "It's awfully dark."

"That bandage across his nose wasn't."

Shelby's eyes narrowed. "That sonofabitch," he snarled, "dooming a hotelful of innocent guests to death, just to even a score."

"Maybe. And maybe there's more to it than simply revenge," Bishop said savagely. "In any case, a payback is coming due." He started toward the mouth of the drive. "Let's check the Gusher."

Shelby and Crandon fell in beside him.

Music drifted toward them as they neared the Gusher. A drunken boomer careened out from the batwings, swearing as he stumbled past them and into the street. Whaleson was back behind the counter again, looking as if he'd sprouted out of the wood like a giant mushroom. He was smoking another torpedo cigar, which he tilted ceiling-ward when he saw them approaching.

"What'll you be having, boys?"

"Jiggs," Crandon said tersely. "On the rocks."

"Sorry, but he ain't here right now."

"Where is he?"

Whaleson shrugged phlegmatically.

Anger roiled through Bishop. Leaning across the bar, he yanked the cigar out of Whaleson's mouth and stubbed its burning ember into the back of his hand. "Where is Jiggs?"

Whaleson let out a gasp and snatched back his hand. Bishop drew his revolver and laid its barrel over the rim of the counter. "If you want," he said through clenched teeth, "I'll finish the job me 'n' Jiggs started on your joint. Now where the goddamn is he?"

"I fired him," Whaleson answered, his piggish eyes glistening behind rolls of fat. "It's one thing for my bouncers to get whupped. It's another to pick fights, and then not show up for work afterward."

"He hasn't been in since we left?"

"A few minutes ago, just long enough for me to pay him off a night's wages, and then he left. In a hurry, too."

"Where? Did he say?"

"Nope. Maybe on a bender, though I kind of doubt that, the way he was." Whaleson rubbed the reddening welt on his hand. "Or maybe like I told you before, back to Cache Springs Ranch."

"Okay, Whale," Crandon said. "Much obliged."

"Sorry about the hand," Bishop added. "You could've saved yourself the hassle, though, if you'd volunteered the information."

"Why? I don't owe you nothing either."

Outside the Gusher again, they paused and Shelby asked, "What's next? Are we going to shake down all the tents and cribs?"

Bishop rubbed his jaw. "I think we'll look up Sedgewick."

"Sounds fine by me," Crandon said.

"You better stay, Em. You're not armed."

"I will be, soon's we get back to the hotel."

"I still figure you can do more good here. You spoke of being tied in with a bunch of wildcatters, didn't you? D'you think you could round up some of them who're good with fists and clubs and who you trust?"

"They're all good and they're all trustworthy. So?"

"So, the two of us can handle Jiggs if we overtake him before he can get to Cache Springs. But if he reaches the ranch safely, it's going to take a lot more muscle than just the three of us to bring him back. Besides, this is only a guess of mine. He easily could still be around, drinking or hiding or both. You and your men could spread out and cover this town in short order, while we're gone."

Crandon yielded to the argument, if reluctantly. "Well . . . it's worth a try. But listen, if you two aren't back lickety-split soon . . ."

"Yeah?"

"We're going to come riding after you."

CHAPTER 8

Returning to the Grand National, Bishop and Shelby hastily saddled their mounts in the hotel stable and once again took to the street. Impatiently they pushed through the crowds, and, when they reached the open road, they let their horses run. Rested and fed, Bishop's chestnut gelding was anxious to stretch its legs, and Shelby's swaybacked mare kept pace with it all the way.

"I know what you're thinking," Shelby yelled over the galloping hoofs. "You're thinking Sedgewick's the man behind Jiggs."

"I'm thinking more'n that," Bishop shouted back. "He could be the brains behind this whole goddamn gang that's got everyone stumped."

"But Em said he'd been buying openly—"

"A smoke screen to throw off suspicion. Just like him, firing Jiggs so he wouldn't be blamed when Jiggs did us in."

"*Tried* to do us in, you mean, and I want to catch Jiggs as much as you do. But assuming you're right, Matt, and Jiggs and Sedgewick are tied in, how can that help clear us of the Lowensburg killing?"

"I've got an idea about that, too."

"Hope so, because the rest of it fits. Fits real well."

"Almost too well," Bishop conceded. "Like it was made to order."

They continued along the same trail they'd ridden that morning. Less than a day had passed since they'd been unceremoniously dragged into Torment and jailed, but it seemed more like a century, so much had been happening. And in a very real sense, Bishop felt, their arrival had been the spark that had caused it all to happen. If only unwittingly, he and Shelby were the needle lancing the boil that had been festering here. And now they had to drain it, to put an end to it.

Scudding clouds hid much of the moon, but flames from flaring wellheads illuminated the surrounding prairie like torches lit by giant sentries. Far ahead could be seen the outline of Lowensburg's dead oil rig and the dark silhouette of the ridge; and beyond that, out of view, would be the fork that must lead to Cache Springs. Much of the trail was also concealed, where it curved around boulders or dipped into black depressions; but even so, Bishop thought there should have been some sign of Jiggs by now—some sound, some blur of motion in the otherwise still landscape. There was nothing. He began to worry that perhaps he'd figured wrong, that Jiggs had fled in some other direction, or had stayed in Torment, perhaps waiting for another chance at them. He'd latched onto this theory of Jiggs returning to Sedgewick because it made sense out of the few facts he'd learned. But it was, after all, merely a theory. . . .

They rounded a bend by an outcropping of rock. Ahead, the trail straddled a wide, shallow bowl of oil-splashed scrub-brush and pools of tarry waste. Directly in front of them, though, and half-parked on the shoulder abutting the outcropping was the Locomobile.

Sedgewick's prized vehicle was tilted at a crazy angle, its left front hub missing its spoked wheel, and its bare axle propped up on a jack. Standing in the middle of the trail, alongside his car, Sedgewick was berating his chauffeur, who in his white smock was trying to remove the tire from the rim with a crowbar-like iron.

"Must've been a flat," Shelby said.

Which must be akin to a horse throwing a shoe, Bishop thought peripherally as they reined in, startling Sedgewick and the chauffeur. Dismounting, revolver cocked, he demanded: "Where is Jiggs?"

Sedgewick, quick to recover, stiffened indignantly. "So they were right about you two. Not only murderers, but bandits as well. Common highwaymen. Well, do your worst, but I'm not carrying any–"

"Goddamnit," Bishop cut in with a snarl. "Where's Jiggs?"

"Working at the Gusher, last I heard, but you won't get a cent–"

"He must've passed you. You must've seen him."

"No, he hasn't. And no, I haven't since I left Torment."

"He's lying, Matt. He's stalling so Jiggs can get away."

"I'm thinking maybe not," Bishop told Shelby, struck by the tone of genuine outrage in Sedgewick's voice. Holstering his revolver, he said, "I'm thinking maybe I figured wrong. Oh, there's a tie-in, alright, but not tween Jiggs and him. It's tween Jiggs and–"

". . . somebody who don't want it noised about," finished a voice from the outcropping of rock beside them. "Now, none of you move."

Bishop recognized the grating deadliness of this voice. He turned slightly in defiance of the order and glimpsed Jiggs easing out from behind cover, training a revolver straight at them.

"A trap!" Shelby blurted. "And Sedgewick was the decoy."

"No," Bishop said curtly, "it's a trap to snare Sedgewick too. To make it appear like he's the ringleader, like I've been suspicioning."

"Not bad guessing, for a senile old fool," Jiggs retorted mockingly. "Can you guess what's going to happen to you all next?"

"We're going to be silenced."

"I don't understand, Matt. If it ain't Sedgewick, who–"

"How dare you accuse me," Sedgewick barked. "And you, Jiggs, put that pistol down. How can shooting us gain you anything?"

"Ask the clever one," Jiggs sneered. "He can tell you."

"It's simple, Jiggs, like you are," Bishop replied, clenching his teeth. "You're secretly working for the gang, along with God only knows how many other gun thugs. You tried having us blamed for Lowensburg's death, and then tried killing us and Em Crandon to get control of the holdings Em put up for our bail. But all you've managed to do is stir up a big loud stink—a stink that can only be calmed if it looks like a gang is no more, and its leader has met a timely fate."

Dawning came to Shelby. "So that's why he's going to shoot Sedgewick! And us, too, 'cept we can't be left here. He'll hafta bury us out there someplace, so it'd seem like we did Sedgewick in and then vamoosed. Then Em'll wind up losing his bond after all."

Sedgewick was staring venomously at Jiggs, his face purpling with rancor. "How could you. Selling out your own ranch—"

"You sold out to oil!" Jiggs snarled. "I was happy just as I was, ramrodding a fine outfit, and then you horned in. You with your fancy-Dan ways and snooty airs, and contempt for all Angus Donovan ever worked and fought for. You did it first, you greedy bastard, and I got to thinking that if you could, why couldn't I."

"You're rotten." And utterly heedless of the revolver aimed at him, Sedgewick started for Jiggs. "You're rotten to the core."

"Stay back!" Shelby shouted in warning.

"Stay back yourself," Sedgewick croaked, taking another step forward. "He's got to be made to pay, be made to pay in full."

Jiggs laughed, notching the hammer of his revolver with an audible click, the cold grin on his face making it clear he was eager to squeeze the trigger the rest of the way. Bishop and Shelby stood frozen in the split second, too close to the insanely advancing Sedgewick to take advantage of the diversion he was creating. But the chauffeur, who had been cowering on the ground next to the wheel rim, reacted with unexpected courage, or perhaps with the same addled hysteria that was gripping his boss. For suddenly, without warning, he scooped up the tire iron and flung it at Jiggs.

The tire iron sailed harmlessly by its target, but Jiggs, distracted, swung his revolver to cover the chauffeur. The chauffeur, whimpering, began scuttling under the Locomobile, and Jiggs, realizing it was a mistake, brought the muzzle back to bear on the other three.

Yet his momentary lapse had been enough. Bishop was used to making up his mind fast, and his right hand blurred in a draw even as Jiggs was leveling his aim and firing.

The twin explosions came almost as one. Bishop felt the sharp burn of lead grazing the side of his neck and saw Jiggs stagger back and drop his revolver, blood welling from his right shoulder. Before he could see whether another shot was needed, Sedgewick was blocking his line of fire, attacking Jiggs with pummeling fists.

"Brutalizing, murdering, all for just money!" Sedgewick was raving, while Jiggs was howling from the fists battering his chest and wounded shoulder. They swayed together on the shoulder of the trail across from the rocks, then Sedgewick managed to hit an especially painful spot, and Jiggs retreated wincing, losing his balance and falling with a backflop into the oozing black muck, which edged that side of the trail. Sedgewick would have followed Jiggs, had not Shelby been in time to grab him and haul him upright.

"Let me go," the arrogantly cultured Sedgewick panted, straining with feral killer instinct to reach Jiggs. "He needs extermination. With my bare hands, if I have to. Don't stop me now."

"He's much too valuable alive," Bishop said to placate Sedgewick, watching Jiggs struggle in the morass, dazed and groggy. "Without Jiggs, we can't prove a case against the rest of the gang."

The words were scarcely out of his mouth, when a rifle cracked from the surrounding high ground. Bishop felt the bullet nick the crown of his hat, nearly lifting it from his head, then heard it puncture the slab metal side of the Locomobile. He swiveled to bring his revolver up to bear, when the rifle roared twice more.

"Goddamn, get down!" he shouted, diving to join the chauffeur under the car, while Shelby and Sedgewick ducked behind the rear fender.

The rifle set up a peppering salvo around them, and now he could hear above its flat bursts echoing down from the boulders the muffled wails of Sedgewick bemoaning the damage being inflicted on his auto. He fired back a few times, more to prove they were not lying there defenseless than at any visible target. Then, as abruptly as it had begun, the rifle ceased firing, and somewhere high off to the right, the sound of a galloping horse rose and faded into the distance.

"Matt?" Shelby called. "You okay?"

"Yeah." Leaving the chauffeur still quaking in a fetal position, Bishop wriggled out from beneath the undercarriage. "Reckon whoever the bushwhacker was, he's hightailed it now," he said, joining Shelby and Sedgewick by the running board. "He was the other half."

"Other half?" Sedgewick asked.

"Of the trap," Bishop explained. "Jiggs was the point man, but the other must've been sent as insurance, as the cleanup man."

"Well, they didn't silence us," Shelby said, gesturing toward Jiggs, who lay sprawling in the oil waste, wearing a jagged hole where his ear had been. "But Jiggs sure got shut up by his ambushin' pal."

Sedgewick glanced, shuddering, from where he was inspecting the bullet holes in his car, and sighed, "There went our proof."

"We ain't going to need much proof," Bishop growled. "Sedgewick, can you ride anything besides this here Loco-ed-mobile?"

Sedgewick reared feistily. "I'm a champion polo player."

"I might've known. Well, then let's go fetch Jiggs's horse—it's got to be ground-reined around here close by—and we'll head back to town. Your driver can finish fixing that tire by his lonesome."

"Excellent idea. The sheriff should be notified."

Bishop grimaced a little, seeing Sedgewick's features settling back in their old law-abiding, virtuous mold. But Bishop had done too much drifting through too many strange, often perilous places for that; he'd learned that the law couldn't always operate the way it should, and he hoped that after this bitter little lesson, Sedgewick would also agree that there were times when brute force was more effective in the application of swift, sure justice. Such a time was coming due.

"I had," he drawled softly, "something more direct in mind."

CHAPTER 9

"Unbelievable!" Emmett Crandon snorted after he'd heard their report. "If you weren't here to confirm it, Lorenzo, I'd swear Matt and Harold had been on a bender and were hallucinating it all."

"It's gospel, Em," Sedgewick said with fiery determination. "I'll vouch by the Bible that if it hadn't been for these two—"

"And your driver," Shelby added.

"Ah yes, and Pettibone. He's earned a nice raise, poor chap. But I'm ready to vouch on any Bible you give me that if it hadn't been for them, Jiggs would have succeeded in his murderous scheme."

"Not his scheme," Bishop said. "It was Whaleson's."

"Whale?" Crandon gasped. "Matt, you must be mistaken—"

"Just add it up," Bishop cut in tersely. "Who else other than you, Em, knew where we were heading? Only the fat man who suggested that direction. He must've been hiding Jiggs all along."

"Sure, so instead of us chasing Jiggs," Shelby said, "Whale sent Jiggs and that other man out to waylay us. It all fits."

"No," Sedgewick argued. "He didn't know I'd have a flat."

"He didn't have to," Shelby insisted. "He'd planned a neat if bloody frame, one that'd work whenever and wherever we might catch up and confront you. Your flat tire was only a piece of luck for him that Jiggs figured on taking advantage of."

"Circumstantial," Crandon said. "We could've been overheard."

Bishop shook his head. "Think, Em, who else is set up to

know when 'n' where to have his gang strike? Only the fat man who leans on his bar counting the money that flows in; money that's chicken feed compared to the big profits he rakes in through using the information that also pours in. That's his real business. The Royal Gusher's merely a blind."

"Well . . . supposin' you're right? What'll we do?"

"Simple. We put that slob outa business."

They were standing in the lobby of the Grand National, surrounded by the dozen hardy wildcatters Crandon had collected while Bishop and Shelby had been hunting Jiggs. The 'catters listened with terse-lipped anger, some of them still unconvinced, but most voicing their thoughts in stern agreement with Bishop and spoiling for a fight.

"If it's true," one of them said, "Whale'll be making tracks out o' town pronto. He must know by now that we know."

"But the man who shot Jiggs must've also reported back by now," Shelby said. "So Whale also must know that Jiggs is dead."

"So what?"

Bishop rubbed his jaw. "Yeah, good point, Harold. Without Jiggs, Whale'll realize we don't have any solid proof against him."

"So we can't have him arrested, is that it?"

"I bet he thinks we ain't got the guts to do anything else about it," another wildcatter yelled. "He's sitting sassy, laughing at us."

"Is that your brand of law, Sedgewick?"

"He'd certainly laugh us out of court, I grant you that," Sedgewick retorted heatedly. "And I grant you that I hired our sheriff. But MacGrueder is his own man. Unfortunately, he's also his *only* man, and you all know how the Gusher is packed with Whale's hired plug-uglies. I plan to wire Oklahoma City for extra deputies, but in the meantime, I feel we've got to act to protect ourselves."

"How?"

"Hit him first, and hit him hard!"

"That's it! Close down the Gusher, permanently!"

"Nail him to the door and do it now, tonight!"

The wildcatters roared with whipped-up enthusiasm, quieting only when Crandon waved his arms. "I got you men into this, just like I got you to pool your oil with Casino," he told them, staring at each one in turn. "So if we do go down there now, we go together, as Casino. And I'll tell you something else: whatever the outcome, tomorrow I'm going to start turning Casino into a corporation, one in which you'll all have a share—literally—because we're going to issue stock and distribute it to you according to the value of your operations. And that goes for every man jack here, by Hades it does!"

"Now, there's something really worth fighting for!"

"Aye, if Casino's to prosper, we'll have to scrub Whaleson!"

"You've got my good right arm, Em. Lead the way!"

The improvised squad of brawny men trooped out of the hotel and down the street. The sputtering lamps in front of the tents cast their advance in weaving shadows, and the prairie breeze tugged at their clothing with a slight yet insistent force. The men clutched an assortment of clubs made from furniture legs and sawn billiard cues; a few carried lengths of choker chain or windlass cable; and one teamster-turned-wildcatter gripped the lead-shot handle of a coiled blacksnake whip in his massive fist. Those with handguns or long-bladed knives kept them safely tucked away, to be used only in case of dire emergency. This was to be a purging, not a massacre.

Just before they reached the Gusher, Sheriff MacGrueder stepped out from across the street and cut across to intercept Sedgewick. "Your chauffeur just arrived, Lorenzo, driving on three wheels."

"He disobeyed me. He was supposed to head for the ranch."

"Loyalty is uncommon enough, Lorenzo. Don't put him down for it." MacGrueder drew into step with Sedgewick, glancing about at Crandon, Bishop, Shelby, and the phalanx of determined wildcatters behind them. "You shouldn't be doing this, and you know it. It's against the law."

"Depends on which law you're meaning, Mac."

"The law you hired me to enforce, Lorenzo."

"Then deputize me—all of us—or arrest us."

"I ain't going to do neither. You're after Whale, right?"

"Pettibone couldn't have told you that. He didn't know."

"No, but he told me enough, and I figured the rest, same as you must've done. Now, listen, I want you to let me do the talking."

"You might as well save your breath," Sedgewick said, and he left it at that. And Bishop suddenly felt a warming toward this pompous tenderfoot. Sedgewick might yet come to terms with this rough-justice world out here, Bishop thought; give him time, but he wasn't as stiff-necked and narrow-minded as he first appeared.

There was the usual knot of barflies floating around the entrance to the Gusher. The same noisy bedlam thundered from within, but silence fell as the men approached, the barflies yielding and drawing aside. The men entered in a narrow, hushed corridor formed by the customers; it was more eloquent than all the shouts and curses of moments before.

Whaleson stood motionless behind the bar. He flicked his gaze out over the bouncers and other mean-looking men who were stationed among the crowd; then he turned his attention back to the wildcatters, his expression as though he were watching a group of strangers arriving for drinks and some fun.

"Evening, Sheriff," he said amiably. "Evening, boys."

"You're under arrest," MacGrueder said, low and hard.

"Anything in particular, or are you just fishing?"

"Jiggs is alive, Whale. Sedgewick's driver brought him in, and he's over at the doc's, spilling to save his neck." Right then, hearing MacGrueder, Bishop decided never, ever, to play poker with any man who could bluff so convincingly. "We've got you dead to rights."

"For what, Sheriff? I still demand to know."

MacGrueder hesitated, not really having any charge he could

make stick. So with nothing to lose, Bishop pulled a bluff of his own.

"For murdering Sy Lowensburg, among others. Jiggs confessed to being hired by you to kill Lowensburg, so you could get his oil well."

"Delirium, or because I fired him. Jiggs is lying."

"He ain't got no reason to. He 'fessed how he killed Lowensburg this morning, while he was on his way from the ranch into town." And Bishop added with a certain bitter malice, "Y'know, when he told the sheriff he'd seen Lowensburg waving to him, he hadn't lied. He'd just forgotten to add he'd left Lowensburg waving from the end of a noose."

For a long moment there were no sounds other than the seething of the kerosene lanterns on the wagon-wheel chandeliers. Then Whaleson said unemotionally, "Hated like hell to put him under, but Sy refused to reason. I had him mousetrapped; I offered him a fair price."

"Alright, Whale, come with me," MacGrueder said, after a sidelong glance at Bishop. "Either peaceably or feet first, but come on."

"I'll make a deal with you," Whaleson said, looking more at Crandon and Sedgewick than MacGrueder. "Maybe Jiggs will live and maybe he won't, maybe you have a case and maybe you don't, but I'm sure you'd prefer not to have the bloodshed it'll take to bring me in. Give me until tomorrow night, and I promise never to come back here."

"You've got till right this minute," MacGrueder snapped.

Whaleson shook his head, slowly and seemingly with profound regret. "Till sundown tomorrow, as the old gunslingers used to say."

"By then," Bishop said furiously, "he'll be out of Oklahoma with all the leases and property he's stolen and murdered for."

"And we'll never get near him again," one of the more hot-tempered wildcatters shouted. "Your minute is all used up, Whale!"

There was a sudden smack of fist upon flesh, as one of

Whaleson's bouncers moved and dealt the firebrand a blow to the chin. Another wildcatter cried out, "Did you see that, fellows? Let's sweep this damn joint to the floorboards and enough of this idle chitchat!"

Sheriff MacGrueder's protests were lost in the surge of voices and feet as the wildcatters released their fury and vengeance. They burst among the crowd, charging toward Whaleson, overtaking the bouncers and hired thugs—cue sticks, table legs, chains, and that whip swinging and lashing and connecting with various skulls and bodies.

Pandemonium erupted inside the tightly packed saloon. Gamblers, girls, and customers scurried like mice; tables, chairs, cards, and dice went over and were trampled underfoot. The bouncers and thugs smashed into the wildcatters with their own brand of billy clubs and brass knuckles. A man collapsed from a concussion on the head, another took a sideswipe across the face that sent him staggering, blinded. The wildcatters pressed on, mixing with the defenders in a swirling, savage melee, that was being joined now by some of the patrons, half of whom were incensed to hear of Whaleson's duplicity, and the other half who didn't give a damn about the saloon owner's crimes, but who were ripe to defend their right for a good time without interference.

Bishop, like the wildcatters around him, was intent on capturing Whaleson. A bartender loomed in his path. Bishop grabbed the man's wrist with his right hand and yanked down viciously, until their faces were merely inches apart. Then Bishop kneed the bartender in the crotch, and the bartender reeled back until his shoulders hit the counter. The heavy bar seemed to shift under the impact as the bartender went over it headfirst and fell to the planks behind it.

Bishop sprang onto the counter only to meet a bouncer swinging a hardwood club. He kicked the bouncer in the face and jumped down behind the bar only to confront the bartender again. The bartender had pulled a loaded sawed-off shotgun from under the counter, and he fired one of its twin barrels, shattering a row of glasses lined on the bar. Bishop snatched up a whiskey bottle from behind the bar and crunched it down on the bartender before he could discharge the second barrel. The bottle broke, leaving Bishop with a broken-glass neck in his fist. It only seemed to enrage the bartender, who reared to fire again, bellowing and half-blinded by the whiskey.

Bishop thrust the neck of the bottle into the man's face, and the second blast flew high over his shoulder, into one of the chandeliers. It severed the cord, sending the chandelier plummeting to the floor, where it struck in a cascade of glass, kerosene, and flame.

Bishop lurched from behind the bar, feeling sick amid the stench of blood and fuel oil and cheap liquor. He stumbled toward the rear of the saloon, seeing that Whaleson was no longer involved in the brawl—and he also glimpsed that the fallen chandelier had spewed fire in licking tendrils across the floor, igniting the wooden tables and chairs, and smoldering around the hem of the heavy cloth curtains.

"Out!" Bishop shouted. "Fire!"

His warnings were drowned in the raucous tumult. With fists, elbows, and knees, he fought his way to Crandon, grabbed him by the arm and yelled, "Get your men out of here! The place is on fire!"

Crandon drew the revolver he'd stuffed in his belt, the blast of the old black-powder .44 like a momentary brake on the swirling battle. In the comparative silence, both he and Bishop bellowed at the top of their lungs, "Out! Out, the Gusher is on fire! Everyone out!"

With the percentage girls squealing and the customers babbling, everybody, including the wildcatters, smashed toward the entrance. The panicked mob tumbled over and around Bishop, but he suddenly felt the bee sting of another sort of pain slice across his shoulder, not far from where his neck had been grazed by the bullet Jiggs had fired.

Whirling, he spotted Whaleson standing partially up the

staircase leading to the mezzanine. Whaleson was pointing a smoking .32 hammerless revolver and was looking at Bishop with a twisted, almost dreamy smile.

"I hate you," Whaleson said, and fired again.

Bishop ducked. The bullet struck a beer keg, sending a stream sluicing through the air. Bishop launched himself up the stairs, and using his own revolver, pistol-whipped Whaleson's wrist. The Smith & Wesson pocket pistol dropped clattering to the steps. Bishop retrieved it and began backing down the steps. "Okay, fatso, come with me."

They were now almost alone in the burning saloon, where overturned tables and chairs were crackling ablaze, hinting of the complete incineration to come. Flames laved the dining room archway with voracious tongues, the fire spreading through the old dry structure with amazing speed, smoke billowing around them in a dense, choking fog.

"The Gusher will be ashes in less than an hour," Bishop said. "There'll be nothing left but cinders to remember it by, and with it, all traces of what you schemed and ordered carried out from here."

"I should've killed you."

"Goddamnit, you tried hard enough."

"Now everything is gone and you're to blame." Whaleson glanced down past Bishop into the saloon. Bishop, wondering if Whaleson was staring at something in particular, glanced fleetingly over his shoulder. And in that instant, Whaleson pivoted and leaped up the remaining steps, staggering out onto the mezzanine. "My office," he cried in a hoarse voice. "All my records, all my leases, I can't let them burn. . . ."

"What the goddamn are you doing?" Bishop yelled.

If Whaleson heard, he didn't care. Fire poured out, gnawing at the supports and roof timbers, enveloping the railing and flooring of the mezzanine. Through this furnace, Whaleson lunged to a door, evidently the door to his office, and, though it appeared to be locked, he tried forcing his body to crush it open, the entire mezzanine now dissolving around him in a vortex of flame. The roof came down and drove sheets of fire downward before it, and Whaleson abruptly vanished in it without another sound, not even a cry or whimper.

The collapsing blast blew Bishop down the staircase, and his legs buckled. His clothing was beginning to singe, but he beat off the flames and dragged himself, dazed, and crawled toward the entrance. Reaching the street, he pushed himself upright, wanting to walk those last few feet. Again his legs gave way, only now hands gripped him, and he heard Shelby's anxious voice and Crandon's wild demanding shout, "Get him back! Back before the whole damn joint blows!"

Bishop watched from the sidelines as the wildcatters pressed the crowds clear of the disintegrating building, while others poured water on the adjacent tents to prevent them from igniting. Within minutes the fire had totally engulfed the saloon; in less than an hour, as Bishop had prophesied, The Royal Gusher was merely a smoking heap where nothing remained that was recognizable. Somewhere in that holocaust was Whaleson, cremated along with everything else he had lied and cheated and stolen and murdered for. Gone, all gone.

Bishop, supported by Shelby and Crandon, joined Sedgewick and the wildcatters as they started up the street again. His left arm was limp and blood was trickling from a bullet gash along his shoulder. "Only nicked along the bone," he kept saying. "I'm fine, just fine."

They came upon Sheriff MacGrueder, who was sitting on the edge of the boardwalk. He looked pale and wan, but he grinned as they approached. He said, "Nothing lost but my brains and my pride."

He had a cracked rib, and a goose egg on his head.

"You'll be the law here for years to come," Sedgewick said.

"God willing," MacGrueder said.

Crandon nodded somberly. "Well, let's get some sleep, all of us. And tomorrow . . ." He paused, looking at Bishop and

Shelby. "Tomorrow, what the hell. I imagine you two will be leaving at sunup."

"Are we?" Shelby asked Bishop.

"You can't," MacGrueder answered instead. "There's the inquest, though it's a formality now. Say, I've been meaning to ask, just how in hell did you know that Whale had hired Jiggs to kill Lowensburg?"

Bishop shrugged. "It had to be. Jiggs was a member of the gang, the gang was after Lowensburg, and Whaleson was the head of the gang. And by Jiggs's own testimony, nobody else had been on the trail. Since we hadn't done it, it had to've been Jiggs when he'd passed by earlier." Then Bishop turned to Crandon. "We can stay longer, Em, if *you* 'd like."

"I'd appreciate it. For a couple of weeks, if you could, until I get this new corporation going and the stock distributed and all that malarkey. And then, if you'd like, I'll come along with you."

Bishop nodded. "I'd a hunch you were angling toward that."

"These are fine people," Crandon struggled to explain, indicating the dispersing wildcatters. "They're family people, settling down and working their property, the way I did years ago when me and Victoria came to Torment and started Casino. When this corporation gets running, it'll be their organization, their wells, that'll bind them to this area and let them grow. Theirs, Matt, not mine. Not me."

"And you, Em?"

"I've had my day. And it's not my way of life any longer, but I haven't had any reason to realize that until you and Harold came. I haven't had any reason to live until now. Can you understand?"

"Don't matter if we do or not, Em," Bishop replied gently. "The only thing that matters is that you do, that's all."

He gave one last backward glance along the street. The breeze stirred the ashes that had once been The Royal Gusher, and across the plain, he could spy the wellhead flares and hear the distant echoing pop of steam boilers. He pulled his left boot out of the oily gumbo of the streetbed, and discovered a dog turd squished to his heel.

He'd stay for Crandon's sake, Bishop promised himself, even though he had a feeling the next two weeks would be the absolute pits.

CHAPTER 10

Finding the whereabouts of the fourth old bank robber, Guffy LeRoy, proved to be every bit as difficult as Em Crandon had feared.

It proved to be a seven-month pain in the ass.

The trio began their hunt where they had left Guffy LeRoy a quarter of a century before, at the small Colorado hamlet in Naughty Girl Valley. Back then, the crossroads burg had been so unimportant that it had no name of its own—or at least none they'd known about—and it more or less had gone under the same name as the valley. Now they discovered it to be a thriving, bustling community, which, with its blossoming civic pride, had wisely adopted a name less degrading in image. Now Naughty Girl Valley was known as Lovers Junction.

More than the name had changed in twenty-five years. The shed-like barn, where long ago Guffy had lain hidden with his wounded leg, had been replaced by the rectory of the First Evangelical Church of the Four-Square Gospel. Where the church vestry now was had been the cabin in which had lived the veterinarian—that very bribable, very alcoholic animal sawbones who'd agreed to treat Guffy's festering leg and give him a safe haven in which to recuperate—for a price.

Bishop, Shelby, and Crandon had not wanted to leave Guffy, but Guffy had insisted. It had been his poor luck to've been winged by a bullet during the bank heist, and after the long, leather-pounding ride up from Arizona, he'd realized he couldn't go any further; he needed rest and treatment, but not the guilt of knowing he was responsible for their capture. At the time, they had no way to tell how successful their getaway had been, so despite some questioning of Doc Frobisher's abilities, they had given Guffy his share of the take, and had continued their mad dash up into Nebraska, where they had split company.

Until now. And now the three found that the Naughty Girl Valley they remembered was gone; the veterinarian's shed and cabin were gone; and boozy Doc Frobisher was gone too, having a decade before been bitten by a crazed sow and killed by infection. With perseverance, however, they located one of the original residents, a certain Widow Pomfret, who dimly recalled an "ely-gant young gennleman" who'd stayed at Doc Frobisher's right around the time in question. The gentleman had walked with a noticeable limp in his left leg, sometimes stumbling, more often swinging out his left leg as though he couldn't bend it.

Enthused, the three persuaded Widow Pomfret to riffle through her old diaries, long since relegated to the bottom of storage trunks. All atwitter from their attention, Widow Pomfret soon unearthed the passages about the gentleman visitor, who was certainly the only noteworthy item in that otherwise news-barren time and place. The gentleman had said his name was Augustan Underwood—just the sort of fancy handle Guffy would pick for an alias—and he had purchased and had sent down from Pueblo at great expense a shiny new surrey with a team of dappled grays—which also would've fit Guffy, the three thought, him having the inclination and the loot to pull ostentatious stunts like that.

So Guffy LeRoy had healed and left Naughty Girl Valley in style, as a high-tone gent called Augustan Underwood. But to where?

It took them two months to learn where. After doggedly tracing in ever-widening circles, checking all the newspaper files and public records they came across, they found where an Augustan Underwood had taken up a section of land in Wyoming, brought in some shorthorn breeders, and started ranching. He'd done well, according to the reports. By about the same time as Doc Frobisher contracted pig fever, Augustan Underwood was turning off two hundred yearlings of beef a year, some running close to a thousand pounds. And he was engaged to marry the daughter of an important cowman downstate.

Then the Central & Northwestern Railway came through. And, according to old newspaper accounts, court documents, and a couple of retired lawyers who'd been involved, the C&NW demanded Underwood vacate "their" land. Evidently, Underwood had never made his proof; had never even thought about it until he kicked the railroad people off his ranch and went down to the land office. Then and there he found the railroad was contesting his filing on the grounds that his house was over the line—on another man's quarter section. It proved to be right; Underwood lost his case and his entire outfit with it—and his fiancée, when it turned out he no longer had any rich future.

Once again Augustan Underwood vanished, this time the only clue being newspaper articles quoting him as saying he was giving up ranching forever and would make his next fortune prospecting up in the Black Hills. So Bishop, Shelby, and Crandon headed for the small group of mountains in northeastern Wyoming and western South Dakota.

Not surprising, they could find no mention of an Augustan Underwood in those 6,000 square miles of watershed forests and mineral-laden rocks. Obviously Guffy LeRoy had dropped that name along with his career as cowman. But, as they tracked persistently around Rapid City, Lead, and Deadwood, they heard of a grizzled, antisocial hermit who walked with a limp and rode a mule with his left leg outstretched. The name of this crusty, misanthropic prospector was Pivotfoot Tubb.

That definitely was not the kind of name, much less occupation, which fit the spoiled hellion they all remembered Guffy LeRoy to be. On the other hand, such a screwing as the railroad gave him would've been enough to sour anyone but a saint. So they began scouring the smaller towns and mining encampments in their effort to locate Pivotfoot Tubb.

Considering the distance they'd already gone, they'd have thought this last patch would've been quick and easy. Instead, it became the longest and most frustrating. They trekked across the hogback ridge, which encircles the Black Hills, and through the Red Valley which extends around the core of this uplift; over the limestone plateau with its enfacing escarpment; along such creeks as the Spearfish, Redwater, Rapid, and Beaver; and eventually into the central area of high ridges, which culminates in the precipitous crags of Harney Peak. And their search, Bishop decided dourly, had to be like the one ol' Timotheus Tighe had made while after him—for wherever they asked, Pivotfoot Tubb either had been or might be again, but never was right then.

Finally, exhausted and frazzled to the point of admitting defeat, they arrived in the mining camp of Ditchwater. Noonday sun beat down upon the sprawling assortment of structures lining the sloping east bank of—logically enough—Ditchwater Creek. Many were saloons. And there were trading posts, an assayer's office, a barber shop, a few agencies for large, outside mining corporations. Others were miners' shacks, unpainted and unkempt, hastily built in the spare time left away from their nearby diggings up the pine-studded gulches and on the smaller tributary streams of the immediate area.

"A gent couldn't die of thirst here," Shelby noted.

"Or starve either, I trust," Bishop added, by way of reminding them it was lunchtime. He kneed his gelding out of the path of a lumbering ore wagon, and reined in by a section of hitching rail in front of a plankboard place called GOOD N PLENTY CAFE. Dismounting, he said, "Speaking of such, let's see if this here is like it says."

Crandon sighed. "Do we have our druthers?"

"Nope," Shelby answered, seeing Bishop step through the door.

Inside the Good n Plenty was a bare-walled room. The front

half had three tables with benches, their wood slick-smooth from wear and grease. The rear part was the kitchen, and standing by its cast-iron cookstove, wiping her hands on a frilly apron, was a tall, gaunt woman who uncommonly resembled Abraham Lincoln without his beard.

"Steak and taters," Bishop called as he sat down.

The woman shook her head. "Sorry, all out."

"Well, if you don't have that," Shelby said, settling beside Bishop, "how about a platter of eggs, sunny-side up, and some chops?"

She shook her head again.

Bishop and Shelby glanced at each other, then over at Crandon, who was now seated across from them. Crandon shrugged and asked the woman, "Then can you rustle up a side of ham and three beers?"

"The beers I got."

"Matt," Shelby said, "let's try someplace else."

But Bishop was not so easily discouraged. "Three beers," he ordered testily, "and three plates of whatever you do have, okay?"

"Mocha fritters, coming up," the woman said with sudden cheerfulness, turning to tend her stove in a clatter of pans and dishes.

"What?" Shelby said aghast. "What was that?"

Now it was Bishop who shrugged, and tried changing the subject by asking the woman, "Ain't this kind of light for luncheon trade?"

"Yep. Business is terrible."

"Can't understand why," Crandon groused.

"You could, if you weren't a stranger," she retorted, using a spatula to turn over a skillet-full of frying corn fritters. "It's all the fault of Capt'n Eloise and his crew of breeds and bandits."

Shelby shook his head. "Captain *Eloise?*"

"You've heard of him?" she asked, dishing the fritters.

"No, but Eloise isn't a very . . . outlawish-sounding name."

"Or brave and heroic, which it's said is why he deserted the army. It's also said he's the only survivor of Little Big Horn, but I think that's bunkum. It's a fact he's familiar with the Black Hills and knows where to hide, I'll grace him that much, I will."

The woman took a can of chocolate syrup from an overhead shelf and began pouring the sauce over the browned fritters. "Back afore Capt'n Eloise," she continued heartily, "there'd be the occasional robbery. Usually the thief was caught and paid dearly. Now there's a rash of 'em, mostly night raids on lonely miners who're supposed to have sizable pokes of dust or nuggets. And always Capt'n Eloise gets away. Oh, sometimes one of his men gets popped, but all of them could be downed and it wouldn't make no difference. Capt'n Eloise would only get another cutthroat crew together in no time. Here, enjoy it."

The last she said while she served the plates of mocha fritters and three bottles of tepid beer. Shelby and Crandon viewed the plates with ill-disguised leeriness. Bishop forked into his chocolate-covered corn fritters without hesitation. "Something wrong?" he asked.

Shelby was more aghast than ever. "Lost my appetite."

Crandon, swallowing, nodded agreement. "I think I have too."

"You won't mind if I eat yours too, then?" Bishop asked, smiling.

And the woman, appearing not to be aware of anything amiss, went on blithely, "Well, Capt'n Eloise must think his crew has to eat like the rest of us, on account last week he held up an entire freight haul, including all my supplies from Hill City. Wiped me bare, he did. Say, pardon me for being nosy, but what's bringing you all to Ditchwater?"

"We're trying to locate an old pal of ours," Crandon said. "A prospector by the name of Pivotfoot Tubb. Maybe you know of him?"

"Pivotfoot? Everybody knows Pivotfoot."

"You wouldn't by some miracle know where he is, would you?"

"Sure. At Hoffnagle's old diggings."

Her answer caused a remarkable, stunning effect on her three customers. Crandon stiffened, and Shelby paused and gawked at her. Bishop's mouth fell wide and his fork suddenly stilled in midair.

The woman frowned. "What's the matter? You sick?"

Crandon recovered first. "No, no. . . . It's just that you're the first person who doesn't know where Pivotfoot was or might be next, but where he is now. Can you show us how to find this place he's at?"

"Sit tight." She went to the counter by the stove, and, upon returning, used the back of an old grocery list to carefully draw a map leading to the Hoffnagle dig. "It's roughly ten miles due west of here, by the stream here, in this little valley. Look for a clearing, about here."

"Thanks," Crandon said. "When did you see him last?"

"Saturday. I staked him to a couple weeks' food; I have been for a while now. Y'see, Hoffnagle quit working a vein that'd thinned out, but Pivotfoot insists a true vein is still there and even claims to've mined it some. He's promised to build me a new restaurant, but I think that's as much bunkum as Capt'n Eloise's tale of fighting alongside Custer." The woman blushed slightly. "I don't care, I feed him anyway. Pivotfoot reminds me a great deal of my third husband."

"My," Shelby commented, trying to be polite as he watched Bishop devouring Crandon's helping. "Have you been married often, ma'am?"

"Twice."

Shelby paled. "Are you about ready to go, Matt?"

"Anytime. Soon's you pay."

"Me? For that? For you?" Shelby choked, spluttering, then growled, "Alright, alright, but only if you promise one thing."

"What?"

"That you won't smoke one of your gawdawful cigars."

Bishop winced. "You sure know how to hurt a guy."

"Believe me, Matt, not as much as you do."

CHAPTER 11

Leaving the town, they began following the woman's map.

That Hoffnagle's dig lay due west was one thing; getting there was a bit more complicated, unless one was a bird. At first they had to head west by southwest, paralleling Ditchwater Creek as it noisily wriggled its way down from the mountains, past the mouths of numerous gulches, sluice boxes, and miner's tents. Then the map directed them to cut off the deep-rutted ore-wagon trail they were riding and take a narrow path that curlicued around in a more northwesterly course. The path was like a narrow, single-file cut, often faint and overgrown, threading through the jagged and gashed land of crags and crevices, close stands of trees, and thickly woven underbrush.

The going was slow and hard, the "roughly ten miles" distance seeming to stretch into a hundred. It wasn't until the first evening shadows started to lengthen in the valleys that the three men crested the last ridge. Together they thrashed their way through the tangle of thorny scrub that coated the summit of the ridge, and halted to peer through a final fringe of branches.

Beyond the ridge fell another slope of stone and forest, plunging to a canyon floor and a rushing, white-water stream. On the near bank of the stream, surrounded by a clearing of tree stumps and chopped brush, stood a wedge tent, looking to be about seven-feet square and made of duck. Between the tent and the stream lay a man's body.

"Mygawd, here we are again," Shelby moaned.

Crandon looked quizzical. "How's that? We haven't been—"

"Not *here,* Em. I'm meaning how me and Matt ran into the

same sort of thing on our way to Torment, finding Lowensburg dead 'n' all."

"There's a difference," Bishop said grimly. "We didn't know Lowensburg, but according to this map, down there is Hoffnagle's dig."

"Guffy!"

They broke into a swinging trot down the slope and galloped like steeplechasers through the obstacle course of stumps and piled brush which cluttered the clearing. Dismounting by the body, they rolled it over on its back and saw where he'd been shot through the chest. They were also relieved to see that in no way could it be Guffy LeRoy after twenty-five years. This man was too young, hardly more than twenty-five himself, though his face was lined and hardened.

"A prospector?" Crandon suggested. "Hoffnagle, maybe?"

"Maybe, but I kinda doubt it," Bishop replied. "He's wearing riding boots, not the low-heeled type a miner would work in. And the calluses on his hands show he's used to roping more'n to digging."

"Well, then, who is he?"

Bishop didn't hazard an opinion right at once. Straightening, he walked slowly around the body and toward the tent, hunkering occasionally to check the ground, where it was scuffed and tamped by the prints of horses and men. The flap of the tent was pulled back, and inside was a shambles, its raw-board flooring torn apart, and everything that could have possibly held anything broken and scattered. From the tent opening, a worn footpath snaked across the clearing to the steep beginnings of the slope, where, bordered by weed-tufted mounds of slag and rubble, was the small, dark mouth of a mine shaft.

"At a guess," Bishop finally replied, as he started along the path, "I'd say that dead fellow begun life as a wrangler, but ended it as a robber, one of a pack of 'em trying to heist whoever lives—or lived—here. He couldn't have been shot for his trouble much earlier than yesterday; him and their tracks are still pretty fresh."

"And we're alone with him, just like we were before," Shelby fretted. "And there's an outlaw bunch roamin' and plunderin', just like before too. I swear, it's like dreaming the same nightmare again."

"Not quite," Crandon said, trying to cheer up Shelby. "We ain't up against the likes of Jiggs and Whaleson this time."

"No," Bishop moaned. "This Capt'n Eloise sounds worse. What's got me bamboozled is how some of the tracks appear to be going in two different directions at once."

"You must be reading confusedly," Crandon said.

"I am, am I?" Bishop snapped, scouting around, then gesturing at a nearby set of boot prints on the path. "Look there. They're small, and you remember how Guffy had small feet. But see how they go along fine, then suddenly one turns to one side or right around backward?"

"Maybe that's how come he earned the moniker 'Pivotfoot.'"

"That still don't explain *why* they go every which way."

"We'll just have to wait to ask Guffy, I suppose."

"If he ain't dead," Shelby added morosely.

Approaching the mine shaft, they saw a battered, iron ore cart tipped on its side and a splintered shingle nailed to a support beam. On the shingle was crudely painted the name "Annabelle."

"That was Guffy's mother's name, as I recall," Crandon said. He rubbed his hand along the inside of the ore cart. "Good color," he declared, inspecting the grit he'd collected under his nails. "The cafe lady told us he'd been bragging about striking a vein."

"Which is probably what attracted the robbers," Bishop said. "They must've torn this place apart looking for his poke, but I don't reckon they found it. If they had, they'd have most likely killed him; and if they'd killed him, they'd have no reason not to leave him right where he dropped, like they did with their own man."

"So either he wasn't here then, or he's hiding out."

"Guffy had to've been here, Em. Otherwise, the dead man don't make no sense. And if he hid, he should've surfaced by now. Besides, there're lots of these tiny, strange tracks down where the robbers were gathered." Bishop rubbed his jaw thoughtfully. "They wouldn't have wanted to stick around long, so I figure they must've taken him with them, hoping to force him to tell where he stashed his poke."

"Bet you're right," Shelby said, "the lousy scum."

"They'll torture him to death afore he talks," Crandon said with growing anger. "You know how stubborn Guffy was, worse'n a mule, and how he could take pain. C'mon, let's get to following them."

Bishop shook his head. "Too late," he replied. "It's almost nightfall now, and we'd only get lost trying to trail them in the dark."

"Yeah, but—"

"Listen, I want to catch up with those bastards as much as you do, Em, but face facts. The best we can do is start tracking as soon as it's light tomorrow morning. In the meantime, let's bury that guy over there and stir up some chuck, and then get a good night's rest."

They got a terrible night's rest. They were utterly convinced by now that Guffy LeRoy and Pivotfoot Tubb were one and the same—the name "Annabelle" and the tiny boot prints, weird as they were, clinched what had been a strong, calculated suspicion lacking corroborative proof. And they were positive that something dreadful had befallen Guffy in the last day or so. But what then had happened to Guffy was still a matter of speculation, and, though Bishop's theory was the best and about the only one they could come up with, it nonetheless resulted in plenty of hashing, cursing debate well into the wee hours.

The most that could be said for their troubled night was that they were able to appropriate some of Guffy's supplies. As a welcome change of menu, they ate and then replenished their stock with what food the robbers hadn't ruined in their hunt. And Shelby replaced his tattered bedroll with a better one, while Crandon helped himself to some rifle-cleaning equipment, and Bishop, finding a crate of short, greasy Giant XX dynamite sticks, stuck a couple in his war bag.

"If that ain't the dumbest," Shelby complained when he saw the capped, fused sticks. "Let a bullet nick them, and you'll blow sky-high."

"Then wipe me off the trees as best you can," Bishop responded. "But we're going after a whole gang of killers, and against them kind of odds, dynamite can sometimes even things better'n shootin' irons."

They left Hoffnagle's dig in the muddy gray hours of false dawn. Mid-morning found them deep in the hill country, with Harney Peak, multicolored and hazy, bulking its high, serrated mass against the western horizon ahead of them. The going was slower than ever, often a crawl, occasionally a complete halt, for no longer was there a set trail to follow, only the spoor of horsemen forging their own path through the wild, remote region. Yet combined, the three pursuers missed little. Every broken branch or matted plant, every faint scratching on rock or marking on ground led them on relentlessly.

By the afternoon of the second day, they were threading their way among the steep foothills of Harney Peak. By now they were haggard from their fatiguing chase, their unshaven faces grizzled and dirty, their clothing, even Shelby's bowler, disreputably wrinkled and torn and smelly with sweat. The canyons continued narrowing as they continued winding higher between the upland cliffs, the forests and thick underbrush thinning to staggered groves and sparse clumps, the daylight barely able to penetrate the ridges and filter down to them.

Eventually they rounded a sharp bend and reined in. Directly before them and extending like the ends of a horseshoe around them, rose the almost vertical face of a massive cliff. Its bouldered slopes were too sheer to root even the hardiest of vegetation, though its uppermost ridges managed to sustain a meager amount of scrub and bracken and gnarled, wind-swept trees. The vast, barren expanse of its sandstone and shale was badly weathered, eroded, and cracked; and from far below, where the three riders surveyed it all in sunless gloom, the whole of the towering cliff surrounding them appeared to be balanced precariously, as if poised on the verge of a huge avalanche.

"Mygawd," Shelby said in a hush, "if anybody tried climbing any part of it, he'd be liable to start the whole mess thundering down."

Crandon nodded, his eyes roving about the base of what seemed to be a boxcar canyon. But he, like the others, knew it couldn't be a dead-end; the gang they were trailing had entered, had no place to hide, and had not turned around, so there had to be another way out.

"Look there," he exclaimed, indicating a shadowy niche ahead of them. "I see a hole in there, like the entrance to a mine shaft."

"Worth checking," Bishop said, as they kneed their horses forward. "But keep your eyes peeled. I've a feeling we're close to–"

He stopped talking in a sudden rush of motion, having glimpsed a wink of light reflecting off a rifle barrel. There was no time for polite warnings; with his left hand, he wrenched Shelby by the shoulder out of the saddle. Even as Shelby was toppling with a startled yelp, Bishop was rising in his stirrups and diving at Crandon, who was riding close on his other side. Tackling Crandon, he dumped them both unceremoniously on the ground, knocking the wind out of Crandon's lungs.

A bullet sheared the air where a second before Shelby had been seated. On its heels came another, which would have punctured Crandon through his spine. The fragile slopes echoed with the harsh cracks of rifle fire, and then all fell quiet again.

"He's hidden behind those boulders on our right," Bishop whispered to his shocked, breathless companions. "Play dead."

For a long, stretching moment they lay perfectly still, straining to hear any signs of the ambusher. The silence continued. . . .

Then softly, cautiously, came the approach of boots. The steps halted a few feet from them, and a voice said, "Get up, you."

Just as cautiously the three straightened. A man stood spraddle-legged, covering them with a rifle cradled in the crook of his arm. The man was big and broad, his mouth wide, and his rough skin sallow. All his teeth were gone except three in front which were brown with tobacco stain. He grinned, showing them. "Now drop your guns."

"Nuts," Bishop retorted. "We'll hang on to them."

The man frowned, aiming directly at Bishop.

Bishop said, "You can get me, but my pals will get you."

The man liked that even less. "Yeah? What're you after?"

"Food and a place to hole up for the night." An injured, whiny note crept into Bishop's voice. "That's all, mister. We're sure not after any trouble. What's the matter with you? We're willing to pay."

"You're going to pay, alright," the man growled, and jabbed with his rifle. "Okay, lead 'em. And I'll be following right in back."

"Sure, sure, anything you say, mister."

Grabbing up their horses' reins, the three began walking slowly toward the mouth of the cave Crandon had spotted. The man strode warily behind them, his rifle poised, ready in case they tried any fast draws. When they had single-filed into the cave, the man called a halt. Balancing his rifle, he fumbled for a match and lit the tar-soaked end of a crude log torch that was propped against one wall. Then he ordered them to move on, their path now illuminated by the flame.

For close to a half hour they trudged, the man grumbling sourly and prodding them along with his rifle. Seeping water trickled down the black walls, odors of decay and excrement stung their nostrils, and swarms of invisible mites pestered them every step of the way. Eventually the endless passage of stone began to tilt upward, a gradual incline adding to their burden. A faint trace of pale light could barely be seen far ahead, and, spying it, the three realized they were following a tunnel that burrowed through the mountain slope.

They continued on, moving closer to the light. Not until they had reached it could they tell precisely where the tunnel exited. But as they stepped from the tunnel mouth, they saw they were entering a large circular clearing, bordered on all sides by high, sheer cliffs. There were a few stands of spindly trees and underbrush, fed by a marshy spring. Studying the terrain, Bishop figured the spring had centuries ago been part of a torrential river system which had, after flooding this natural basin, eroded a sewer through the rock, forming what was now the tunnel and the deep, narrow canyon on the other side.

Near the spring were a number of tents and makeshift lean-tos, campfires and camping paraphernalia, and a rope-enclosed remuda nibbling the sparse grass. Set off to one side were two stone huts. One obviously served as a jail, for its single window was barred and its thick wooden door was secured by a stout crossbar. The other hut had no bars in its window or across its door, but did have a crudely-rigged porch and roof arranged along its front.

Behind Bishop, Shelby, and Crandon, the man told them to wait while he extinguished the torch in the soil. Then he prompted them forward again, toward the rock huts. Other men now started gathering, stopping what they were doing or coming out from their shelters to eye the three strangers with suspicion and malevolence. Seventeen, Bishop counted, and a nastier bunch he'd never seen. They were a motley mix of breed and color, one being a big-bellied Chinaman, two others Greeks, a fourth looking to be Sicilian, a fifth like an Ozark hillbilly, and three more ranging from the café au lait of the Caribbean to the dark blue-black of West-Coast Africa. The rest could have been anything from a combination of Indian and European stock, to the spawn of the Barbary Coast's "alley of a thousand tongues," including one veritable giant of a lout, whose right eye drooped with the weight of a bulbous, grayish-yellow growth.

Yet it was the sight of two other men which locked the attention of Bishop and his companions. Each of the two was sitting in front of his respective hut, one on the ground and the other in a rocking chair. The one on the ground had his back propped against the barred door of the jail hut, and looked like a caricature of Guffy LeRoy.

Appalled, Bishop realized it *was* Guffy LeRoy.

CHAPTER 12

Bishop felt sickened by how changed LeRoy appeared.

The three had to pass the jail hut in order to get to the other one, where the man behind them was prompting them to head. And nearing Guffy LeRoy, Bishop recalled the partner he'd known in Canta Lupe as having been lithe and willowy as a whip, ever laughing, even when he loosed a temper as fiery as his red hair. But now LeRoy's flesh hung in folds, as if grown to accommodate a pudginess which had been worn away by hunger and pain. His great shock of hair was pure white, ghostly white, and his freckles had given way to gorged veins. And his face was humorless, bitter, his eyes red as blazing brands, his mouth a gash. He was wearing no shirt, no hat, only a patched pair of Levi's and a run-over Justin boot. Just one boot.

From mid-thigh on down, his left leg was missing.

Guffy, spotting his three old partners, stared with disbelieving eyes. Then a claw-like hand swept through his hair, and holding on to the door frame, he struggled upright and braced himself, mouth opening.

Fearing he would blurt out his recognition, Bishop gave LeRoy a quick, terse shake of the head. LeRoy caught the warning and clamped his mouth shut. Bishop, trying to cover any notice of his signal, turned and drawled at the man behind, "Who's the cripple? A mascot?"

The man sneered. "Naw, that's what we do with nosy strangers like you, when we don't want them to slip out and leave us."

"I see your point," Crandon said in a choking voice. "A guy can't stray very far, I guess, with one leg and no crutches."

"Oh, Pivotfoot's got another leg," the man said. "Does okay on it, too. That's why Cap' Eloise is holding it, for safekeeping."

Which meant, Bishop reckoned, that the second man, the man resting in the rocking chair on the porch of the second hut, was the notorious Captain Eloise, the self-proclaimed scourge of the Black Hills. And approaching, Bishop could understand how Captain Eloise could recruit and control such a scurvy crew of thugs as this.

A good many thousands of years ago, you could step into any forest and heave a rock into almost any tree, and bring down an exact replica of Captain Eloise—except that the captain was missing a tail and had covered his nakedness with ill-fitting clothes instead of a well-fitting coat of fur. He had a neck resembling a braided hawser the thickness of a telegraph pole, and his balding black hair left the front part of his skull bare and glistening with perspiration. His face had been lumped, kicked, and hash-knifed; and his nose started flat, swiveled left, and then made a reverse right angle.

And, as the captain stood to see what in blazes he was being brought, Bishop noted that his legs were bandied and bowed, his knees sagging from the strain of carrying a tremendous weight. No flab: his forearms, chest, and thighs bulged with muscles upon muscles.

"Yeah, Garth? You're supposed to be guarding," he squeaked.

Squeaked! The high peepish voice coming from Captain Eloise's maw of a mouth was a stunning surprise, a joke cast by ironic fate. But it was equally obvious, Bishop realized, that it was worth one's own life to make mention of it, or even to show a reaction to it.

"Sorry, Cap'," Garth said humbly. "But I either killed them or brought them in, and I figured you might want to hear their say."

"Yeah? Hear them—or their side arms?"

"Whoa there, your honor," Bishop began. "Like we—"

"Captain Eloise," the outlaw leader cut in sharply, proudly, expectantly eyeing his unwelcome guests for signs of recognition.

Bishop merely grinned his soft, amiable grin. "Pleased to meetcha, Capt'n. And like we were telling your sergeant here, we didn't drop by to trade lead. Hell, we didn't even know we were going to drop by here. Fact is, we're trying to avoid dropping by places; we had our fill of such ruckusin' back where we came from."

Captain Eloise sat back down. "Oh yeah? And why's that?"

"Well, that's a kinda long and embarrassing history to relate, Capt'n. Let's leave it at being strangers hereabouts, coming down from Montana way, figuring on heading south. Moving fast and light."

"Yeah? Anybody else with you?"

"Nope. But there was a bunch of hot-trotting gents behind us for a while, eating our dust before we lost 'em outside of Billings."

"These gents, did they happen to be wearing stars?"

Bishop quirked his lips. "There might've been one or two."

Captain Eloise cocked an eyebrow at Garth, and Garth responded with a shrug, saying, "Well, they were alone when I got them, sir."

"Yeah. . . ." Rocking thoughtfully, the captain surveyed their grizzled faces and filthy garb. And if ever he'd seen men on a hell-for-leather dodge from the law, it had to be these three old scoundrels. He scratched his chest through his shirt and asked, "So what do you want from me?"

"Nothing," Bishop countered. "We didn't ask to be drug here and introduced to you at the point of a rifle. And if your lieutenant Garth hadn't had such an itchy trigger finger, we'd have turned around in that canyon and gone our own trail, and never known no different."

"He lies," Garth snarled, beginning to steam and turn scarlet. "Outside there, he told me they're after food and a place to hole up."

"Why, sure I did," Bishop replied, becoming cagey now. "What else could I say with a muzzle poking me in the belly? And it's true enough in its own way; we can use some fresh chow and a safe bunk."

"And we told this Garth fellow we're willing to pay, too," Crandon suddenly interjected. He, like Shelby, had been standing mute while they figured Bishop's drift; and now, seeing that it had a chance to work, he added to it by hauling out a fat roll of banknotes and flashing the wad under Captain Eloise's nose.

"Y'see?" he demanded, and the captain's eyes sparkled as he glimpsed the denomination of the top bill. Crandon, not bothering to explain that the bill was the only one of its kind in the roll, or that the roll contained most all the funds the three had left, repocketed the wad and huffed indignantly, "We're loaded, see. Name your price."

Captain Eloise smiled, though his eyes grew lidded and sly. "I've a notion you're the sort who'll fit in real nicely here. That is, so long as you remember I'm the boss and what I say goes."

"It's your fiddle here, so we'll dance to your tune," Bishop instantly agreed. "Only don't you forget, Capt'n, we know all the tricks and don't aim to be trifled with. There's plenty of you to take us, but we'll sure thin your ranks if it comes down to that."

"You've nothing to fear," the captain replied, and his high-pitched voice fairly purred. "Garth, show 'em where to camp and have their horses staked out with the others. And if they want to buy food or drink, let 'em dicker with the boys. Then get back to guarding."

He gestured dismissively, and Garth motioned for the three to follow him. The horses were unsaddled and placed under the care of one of the Greeks. Then Garth chose a camping area conveniently in the midst of the gang members' shelters, and, though being surrounded that way left them at a serious disadvantage in case of trouble, Bishop and his companions carefully refrained from complaining.

Actually the spot had its good points, in that it allowed them to mingle with the others. And with Captain Eloise having approved of their stay, his men accepted them as a matter of course. One of the blacks sold them biscuits and something that might have been called chili soup. The hulking brute with the eye problem haggled stubbornly over the cost of his "extra special fine corn whiskey," but Crandon, the recent master of oil lease negotiations, reasoned him down to where the price of a jug of Old Thundermug was merely outrageous.

Shelby snagged the jug before Crandon could get his hand on it. "Mygawd, give me water," he rasped, tears streaming down his face from the heat of the green peppers in the chili soup. He took a hefty swig to cool the raging fire in his belly. His face stiffened. He gagged and groped for his bowl of chili again—the lesser of the two evils.

"That good, eh?" Bishop said, slapping Shelby heartily on the back as he swiped the jug for himself. "Over the lips, over the gums, look out stomach, here it comes," he caroled, and swallowed heavily.

Old Thundermug was properly named. It tasted like the dregs of a well-used chamber pot, steaming and burning all the way down, and when it landed in his gut it seemed to shrivel and corrode the lining. His eyes swelled, his cheeks ballooned, and he was sure his teeth were rotting loose in their sockets. "Goddamn sheep dip!" he squawked.

The giant of a man was cackling madly. "Maybe, but it's the best there is in the camp," he chortled. "Here, the next jug's on me, just to prove t'you Anvil Varek's heart is in the right place."

One look at Varek's jaw, and Bishop didn't have to ask how he earned the nickname "Anvil." Another look at the rest of Varek, and Bishop didn't feel like questioning his generous offer of more poison. Besides, he'd regained his breath, and the next sip wasn't so bad, and the next one after that was downright mellowing. Shelby was no longer strangling, and Crandon didn't seem to be affected one way or t'other.

The evening wore on. The three tippled steadily, ignoring the danger. That they were in a trap, and that Captain Eloise and his crew had no intention of letting them leave until they were relieved of their money and quite probably their lives, should have been apparent to them. But if it was, they acted as if they couldn't care less. Any more than they seemed interested when Guffy LeRoy was herded into his cell-like hut, or when night guards were posted by the remuda and tunnel entrance.

Instead, they swapped tall tales with the captain's shifty-eyed mob, regaling, while they drank, with the wild yarn of robbing a bank and riding like hell to escape a posse. It wasn't all a lie: they merely upgraded their Canta Lupe heist by twenty-five years, switched the event to Bozeman, Montana, and changed the names to protect the guilty. It sure told good. And even more wondrous to the men was how these three old farts could swill Anvil Varek's rotgut booze. Varek himself stopped laughing at them, his one good eye widening with amazement. Nobody before had guzzled four jugs of Old Thundermug and still remained conscious, much less coherent!

Along toward midnight, the party began to break up. Some of the men stumbled into their shelters and sacked out snoring. Others wandered over to the Sicilian's tent and started a crap game. Bishop, Shelby, and Crandon lurched off toward their bedrolls, their arms thrown about one another as they warbled half-remembered, bawdy ballads.

Oh, in yonder mossy hollow,
Her tasty oyster throbbed. . . .

Anvil Varek went around collecting his empty jugs, scowling at the unharmonious trio, their off-key rather than off-color singing a painful affront to his ears. He hastened to the dice game as fast as he could, leaving them on their blankets, still serenading the moon.

"He's gone," Crandon said, after they finished a risqué rendition of *I'm an Old Cowpile.* "They're all gone, except for the guards."

"They're suspicious skunks, alright," Bishop murmured, rubbing the palms of his hands over his liquor-fogged eyes. "But I think we convinced them we're what we're pretending to be. Harmless idiots."

"Not surprising," Shelby growled. He rose, stretching with a serious deliberateness, and, swaying slightly, owlishly surveyed the camp by the dingy light of the banked fires. "Our last ditty would've chased away the devil himself; and anyway, who'd reckon we were anything but loco, to be gargling that bootleg shellac of Varek's like we did."

"Well, sober up, 'cause we've plenty to do now."

"Yeah, Matt, but how?" Crandon demanded. "We've got to saddle our horses and one for Guffy; break him out of his hut; and not only pass through the camp, but through the tunnel as well, which is guarded. And somehow steal that fake leg of his, which Garth said Eloise had."

"Yeah, there're too many 'gots,'" Shelby argued.

"The main 'got' is that we've got to get out of here tonight. Our bankroll will run out tomorrow, and then they'll know we've been fooling them, and then–" Bishop sliced his finger graphically across his throat. "Our only chance is to take things one at a time, starting with the remuda. Then we'll snatch Guffy's leg from the captain–who, if you've noticed, is alone in his hut–and release Guffy. As for the tunnel guards, well, count the men in camp and you'll find that no guard on the outside has been posted, just one here on the inside."

"Just!" Crandon groused. "You make it sound easier'n dancing a jig. I hope so, Matt, 'cause you're right, we've got to try. . . ."

Try they did, a short while later. Time first had to be spent for plans and checking weapons; and for the camp to be lulled by night, the men sleeping or playing dice, and the guards wearying of monotonous routine. To Bishop, this was the worst part of any battle, this calm preceding the action. He remained edgy, unable to shake the notion of having to get out, to get this fight over with as swiftly and silently as possible, or risk total collapse of their plans.

When finally they made their move, they had developed a scheme of sorts. Their pockets bulged with short-cut lengths of rope, and Bishop had slipped the dynamite sticks from his war bag into his shirt. Quickly they fashioned crude dummies out of nearby kindling and grass, stuffing their bedrolls to make it appear they were sprawled asleep. It was unfortunate that they'd have to leave their bedrolls and bags behind, but on the other hand, their skins were much more valuable.

They scuttled low across the clearing, keeping well away from the feeble light of the smoldering campfires, gliding through the dark shadows cast by the rear of the shelters. Stealthily they approached the remuda, where the Ozark hillbilly lazily stood sentry, a chaw of tobacco in the side of his mouth. He stiffened like a starched shirt when Crandon and Shelby bored two pistol muzzles into his ribs.

"Open your mouth," Bishop warned him in a low voice, "and you'll be deader'n hell with the lamps out."

The man's knees knocked and spittle seeped down through his wiry beard, as Bishop tied and gagged him with pieces of the cut rope. They dragged him into the middle of the remuda, where he'd be hidden by the horses. Then Shelby, who was the closest in physique to the man, put on the man's hat and began to act as guard—although this time, his duties consisted of nonchalantly saddling four horses.

Leaving Shelby, Bishop and Crandon eased back into the night. Slowly worming their way to Captain Eloise's hut, they dipped into the black shelter of the porch roof, and quietly toed along the front to the door. Then pausing outside the door, they knocked.

All was silent from within.

Bishop knocked again, softly yet insistently.

"Wha . . . ?" came a groggy, sleepy voice.

"Garth," he growled, in a rough imitation. "Sorry, but it's

damn important, Cap'. It's about them bums we took in today."

There was a guttural cursing and the sound of feet padding to the door. There was the rumble of a heavy bar being lifted from its brackets. The door began to open. "Yeah, Garth, this'd better–"

Bishop and Crandon thrust against the door, forcing it wide and sending Captain Eloise stumbling off-balance. Before the captain could regain his logy wits, they were on him, Crandon clutching that great corded neck, Bishop jamming his revolver against that splayed nose.

"Not one bleat outa you," Bishop hissed.

"What–whatnahell!" Captain Eloise snarled. "You sonof–"

The captain started to struggle, but Bishop hit him so hard with his heavy revolver that he sprawled forward onto the floor like a dead toad. They gagged him then and roped his wrists and ankles to a big-bellied stove in one corner.

Crandon closed the door gently, and they set to searching for Guffy's artificial leg. Time was of the essence, yet they couldn't risk lighting a lantern for fear of it being seen through the window. They had to paw through the hut in the darkness, but luckily there wasn't much to it–just a cot, a table, a couple of chairs, a steamer trunk, and the stove. They discovered the leg hanging on the wall by its leather straps, as if it were some sort of exotic decor.

The leg was fashioned out of metal, with a complex system of hinges, springs, and counterweights to operate the joints. It was painted a pale pinkish beige that failed miserably as a flesh tone. Even so, seeing it in his grasp with its sock and other Justin boot still on it, Bishop felt a sense of revulsion as if he was handling a real leg. "What a lousy trick," he growled, hastily wrapping the mechanical leg in the cot's dirty blanket. "Goddamn 'em, I'd like to take all their legs, especially the captain's, and see how they like it."

"Later, Matt," Crandon whispered anxiously, easing open the door and peering out. "C'mon, let's get Guffy's back to him."

They stepped back out onto the porch, noiselessly shutting the door behind them. Then reaching the corner, they were about to slip around the side of the hut, when Crandon tugged Bishop, stopping him.

"The guard," Crandon mouthed. "He's coming."

Now Bishop, hugging flat against the wall of the hut, could see the guard strolling across from the tunnel entrance. At first it appeared he was heading for the hut, but after a couple of breathless moments, it became clear he was angling toward the remuda. "Goddamn," Bishop said. "He'll spot Shelby. Listen, Em, call him over here."

"What?"

"Call the guard to you," Bishop reiterated, sliding around the corner and hunching, hidden, in the shadows. "Whistle at him or something."

Crandon sighed heavily, but, puckering his lips, let out a soft whistle. The guard hesitated, glancing his way. Crandon motioned with his hand, still keeping himself cloaked under the porch roof.

"C'mere," he called in a barely audible voice.

"Whaddyuh want?" the guard asked, squinting.

"Capt'n Eloise was asking about . . ."

"About what?" The guard was almost to the porch now.

Crandon gestured toward the door. "He'll tell you."

The guard muttered an obscenity under his breath, but obligingly turned his attention to where Crandon was pointing. And Bishop rose up behind him and fetched him a hard clout on the head with Guffy's leg.

The guard's hat flattened with a horrendous dent, and quite likely his skull did too, and from inside the mechanical limb came a twanging like that of a harp being plucked. And Bishop had rarely felt so satisfied. "There, Guffy got in a blow," he said, hauling the unconscious guard around the corner. "Hope I didn't hurt the leg."

They tied and gagged the guard on the slight chance he might awaken, then sidled back over to the remuda. Shelby was ready with the horses. The way the remuda and LeRoy's hut were situated, they could lead the horses to the hut without being spotted. That is, if they were very careful, and none of the captain's gang happened to feel the urge to go strolling out and about. Alas, the way the crossbarred door of the hut was situated, anyone trying to open it or come out would be in the direct view and pistol range of the gunmen.

Which meant that LeRoy had to escape via the window.

There was a patter of hoofs in the darkness as the three walked the four mounts to the hut. "Guffy!" Shelby hissed under the window.

"Shut up, lemme sleep, I– What'd you call me?" There was a scuffling, a hopping, and then a fierce face, with red-rimmed eyes and sunken cheeks, appeared at the window and hands clasped the bars.

"Howdy, Guffy," Crandon said quietly.

"Don't quip me, you're all mirages like dyin' folks see in the desert." LeRoy's mouth cracked into a parched grin. "It's great to see you, even here. Doggone, but you haven't changed much, have you?"

"Nor you," Bishop murmured, careful to conceal his lie. "Listen, there's no time to palaver. We're breaking you out and moving on fast. . . . I picked a rangy roan for you," Bishop added.

"Very funny, hah hah. Without both my legs, I'm like a turtle on its back. Go on while you can, pals. I'm going nowhere."

"Catch," Bishop said, and tossed the blanket-wrapped limb between the window bars. LeRoy fielded it, almost tripping and falling, but feeling the familiar shape in the blanket, he tore the wrappings off and held his leg up for inspection. And he laughed. It was a throaty, scornful laugh; yet hearing it, Bishop suddenly recognized the Guffy of old–the Guffy as he remembered him, bloodied by life perhaps, but still unbeaten and unbowed.

"Best bet is to latch onto these bars with a catch rope," LeRoy said, nervously strapping on his leg, his fingers shaking so that he could barely control them. "See if you can yank them out, okay?"

"We already had that in mind," Crandon chuckled.

Swiftly they uncoiled the ropes from their saddles and knotted one to each of three iron bars. Then remounting, they eased into a pull. Hoofs scraped the earth, saddle leather popped, as the hemp ropes pulled snug. "More," Bishop urged, feeling his nerves tighten along with the rope. At any moment, he expected gunfire to blast through the night, to feel a salvo of lead strike its mark. He heard a mumble of voices lifting, but so intent were Captain Eloise's crew with their dice game, that the sounds coming from the hut were ignored.

The bars creaked and began to bend, but not to yield. "By Hades," Crandon said. "We've got to hurry. Let's back and spur."

The three reined in, allowing the ropes to slacken. Then in unison, they heeled their mounts surging forward. The hemp snapped taut, but still the bars refused to give way. Instead, the entire side of the hut collapsed in a rumbling cataract of rock and dust. Two rats scampered panic-stricken for cover, and, coughing, Guffy LeRoy grappled, clawing through the aperture, intent on getting away.

The bars stuck at odd angles up through the rubble. One of them snagged LeRoy's trousers as he crawled. Desperately he tried to untangle himself, as now shouts and whoops echoed from the aroused camp.

"Hurry, goddamnit," Bishop yelled, while the first gunshots erupted. He drew his revolver, preparing to fight. *"Hurry!"*

LeRoy renewed his efforts to dislodge the hooked bar. His pants ripped, a patch of denim remaining spiked to the iron rod as he hobbled frantically over the mound of stone blocks. Tumbling to bare ground, he lurched for the roan in a crazy sort of springing, hopscotching trot. He kept his left leg stiff, his artificial limb making erratic, roundhouse punches in the dirt each time it landed—but it never quite landed the same way twice, because something was screwball with the ankle mechanism, allowing it to swivel freely, much in the same manner as a caster works on the legs of furniture.

Fascinated, Bishop thought fleetingly, So that's why Guffy is known as Pivotfoot. . . . That was all the time he had for such observations, for now LeRoy was seated on his horse. The four were at last together again, and as a team they charged galloping across the weedy clearing and raced for the entrance to the tunnel.

Behind and around them gunfire thundered, bullets whining past them like lead-jacketed hornets. Bending low on their horses, they entered the tunnel, its low, jagged roof scratching their spines. The lengthy passage resounded with their hoof beats and shortly with the clattering noise of other shod horses. The gang was in hot pursuit.

"We should've choused their horses instead of leaving them in that remuda," Shelby complained. "They'll be able to ride us down."

"Not before we can reach the other end," Bishop shouted back.

"Fine! Wonderful! That still leaves that long stretch of canyon before we can hope to ditch them in the hills."

"Then we'll just have to bottle them in the tunnel, Em."

LeRoy swore loudly. "Blast their mangy hides!"

"That," Bishop yelled, "is the general idea. . . ."

Black and blind was the interior of that endless cavern, but spooked by the tumult and shots behind them, the horses sped on, seeming to sense unerringly the route ahead. When eventually they rushed out into the grayer dimness of outside night, Bishop let them run about thirty yards from the tunnel entrance and then called to rein in.

"Hold 'em in there!" he bellowed, his order almost drowned in the uproar of gun blasts and galloping horses as the gang rolled toward them.

The first of Captain Eloise's mob grew visible in the mouth of the tunnel. They were met with a hail of lead, as Shelby, Crandon, and LeRoy crouched behind boulders and aimed at the black hole. Horses screamed and went down, men howled and went with them, some pinned beneath their kicking mounts. The dead and injured piled like bloody cordwood just inside the entrance, but the raging pack behind used it as a barricade, laying down a barrage of withering fire.

The three outside spaced their shots carefully, their only reloads being what Shelby and Crandon carried in their cartridge belts. Their intent was to keep the captain's gang pinned in the tunnel, well aware those brutal killers would never willingly retreat. And their only hope was that Bishop had not entirely gone mad, crazy though he was acting. It was a simple matter of stalling while their ammunition held out. After that, well, it'd been a nice life while it lasted. . . .

Bishop had no intention of allowing their predicament to get that far. Having tossed his revolver to LeRoy, he darted diagonally for the rocks bordering the tunnel. While the others laid down their covering fire, he wormed his way up and around, ever closer, until he was almost in line with the rifle barrels poking out from the entrance.

Squatting, he took one of the sticks of dynamite out from his shirt, and fumbled in his pocket for a sulfur match. He chuckled. It was a genial chuckle, one which grew friendlier while he scratched the match alight and set fire to the short fuse of the stick. He watched the spunk burn halfway, mentally counting the seconds it took, and when he judged it to be ready, he slung it underhand down into the tunnel. He didn't wait around to watch the result.

"Down!" he yelled at the others, scrambling frantically back along the side of the canyon, sending showers of pebbles cascading as he loped from rock to rock. "Eat dirt, fellers, it's about to–"

His warning was lost in the deafening explosion of dynamite. The mouth of the tunnel volcanoed fire and heat and chunks of horses and men as if it were the discharge from some monstrously huge cannon. The blast hit Bishop like a mailed fist, and he felt the earth shiver beneath his feet as the eruption ripped through the narrow chasm's floor. He sailed through the air, skidding when he landed, and tried desperately to protect himself from the pelting rain of sandstone and shale as he picked himself up and continued running.

He could hear the other men yelling, as the detonation died away—his three partners calling in alarm to him; and the bloodthirsty crew in the tunnel wailing and moaning from shock and agony. And then came another sound—an ominous, sundering crack starting high along the crest of the slopes. The dynamite had shattered the delicate internal balance of the canyon, and the steep, rubbled sides groaned and shifted under the altered strain. The upper layers began splintering and gaping wide, shaking loose tons of earth and stone in a tumbling landslide down the banks and over the tunnel entrance.

Shelby, Crandon, and LeRoy ran scurrying for their shying horses, realizing that soon the canyon would be inundated with debris, and that they had to race like hell to avoid being engulfed. Bishop was almost to them. The earth shuddered and danced, throwing him to his knees. He rose and plunged onward, making a sprinting leap into the saddle of his gelding, which would have bolted if Shelby had not been holding it steady by its bridle.

They galloped down the canyon, as its walls caved in behind them in a series of solid tidal waves. Bishop glanced backward, but could see nothing of Captain Eloise's gang through the flood of dust and rolling boulders. Nor could he hear their howling, though howling they surely must be doing—those who were not already dead, that is. The survivors were trapped, if not in the tunnel itself, then in the deep bowl of their camp. They might never get out alive.

Bishop turned then and grinned mirthlessly at his companions. They grinned back. And the four dashed on to safety, feeling no pity or remorse for their harsh actions against that vicious mob.

CHAPTER 13

Their leisurely trip back to Hoffnagle's dig was spent mainly in catching up on the past twenty-five years. That took in a lot of territory, and however else Guffy LeRoy may've changed, he hadn't lost his ability to spin a fine yarn. Naturally the others rose to his challenge, so by the time he'd collected his few remaining belongings and they were on their way to Ditchwater Creek, their reminiscences were beginning to sound a bit more elaborate, if not downright extravagant.

After two full days of fattening up Guffy at the Good n Plenty, and generally celebrating their reunion at various saloons, historical accuracy was definitely on the questionable side, though none of them had the ill manners to query even the most dubious of facts.

On the third morning of their stay in the mining camp, the four were again at the cafe, gathered 'round their favorite table, the one nearest the kitchen. By mutual consent, their old Canta Lupe bank heist was never mentioned, for obvious reasons; nor was their recent destruction of Captain Eloise's gang, all of them leery of the publicity such news would create. And because Guffy was known hereabouts as Pivotfoot Tubb—hereabouts including, in particular, the woman in the kitchen—that is what they called him. Otherwise there were no limitations, and hot air blew in tornado strength.

"I recollect when I was foreman of the Lazy Q, outside Amarillo," Bishop was saying in between mouthfuls, "had me the orneriest, balkiest herd known to man, I did, and at roundup, me'n my crew couldn't move 'em into the loading pens. Swearin' and hittin', even poppin' off a few rounds, wouldn't budge nary a one. 'Matt, I'm ruined if I don't deliver,' Quigley told me, Quigley bein' the owner. 'Matt, you're ramrodding my outfit, you gotta do something, no matter how drastic.'"

Bishop paused, swirling his fork about his dish to emphasize the gravity of the situation. Or perhaps it was to forestall eating any more food. It wasn't another mocha fritter, for which he felt blessed, but since supplies were still at a premium, the best the woman could concoct was something she referred to as a spaghetti enchilada.

"So I have my crew stand back," Bishop continued, "and I go up to the lead steer, a stubborn, curly-horned brute. I give him my mean eye, just to show him who's boss, then I pick him up and haul him bodily into the pen. Well, you na'ar seen such a confused longhorn in all your born days. Afore he can recover, I quick go out and carry in the next nearest cow, and I keep on a-carting till the entire herd is inside. Ol' Quigley gave me a bonus for that, too."

Crandon and Shelby let out low, muffled groans, and from the kitchen came the clatter of a dropped saucepan. Guffy LeRoy said, "Sure sounds like you slung a lotta bull that time, Matt," and he chuckled at his own pun before turning very sober. "Seriously, though, that can't help but remind me of the winter of '97, when I rescued Ophelia Comstock. She of the Comstock Lode family, y'know."

"Load of what?" Bishop quipped to get even.

Guffy ignored him. "Now, that was a winter. Drifts thirty feet high on the levels, gents, and blizzards howlin' through the Sierras when Ophelia, heiress to a fortune, went and got lost. I set to tracking her, like any right-minded humanitarian oughta, and danged if I don't find her trapped on an iceflow, out in the middle of the treacherous Carson River. I plunge in anyhow, only it's so cold that my horse froze solid under me. Luckily, I'd thought ahead and brung me along a canoe paddle, and I was able to row the horse across to her, using its tail like a rudder to steady my course. When I'd rescued her and got her ashore, I lit a fire and thawed out my horse, then rode double with her back to Virginia City."

LeRoy's audience gaped, too flabbergasted to groan. There was a moment of utter silence, broken by the woman stalking from her kitchen.

"No more," she declared, cheeks flushed. "It's almost lunchtime, and I've enough frazzles cooking for my customers without having to stomach such errant tripe. I'll have to ask you to leave, please."

Shelby frowned at LeRoy. "You heard the lady."

"I mean the lot of you," she snapped. "You've roosted here too long as it is. Go away, and preferably stay away a week or two."

Chagrined, the four men paid for their meals and filed meekly out the door. Grouping in the street, Crandon told LeRoy, "Just see what you've done, Guffy, making us all look like old windbag loafers."

"And corrupting that poor lady's mind with outrageous nonsense," Bishop added indignantly. "Why, you should be mortally ashamed."

"Hold on, you ain't got no cause to gang up on me," LeRoy objected. "I can't help it if I spoke only the unvarnished gospel."

"I think I could use some varnish about now." Shelby, his expression pained, rubbed his belly. "I sure could go for something liquified, to tie down and gentle whatever that mess was she fed us."

"Good idea, Harold," Bishop agreed and, with a rumbly belch, led the way into the closest saloon, where he had the bartender set out a bottle. He poured himself a snort and passed the bottle, and when LeRoy filled his shotglass, Bishop raised his drink in a mock toast.

"You should've used this, Guffy, to thaw out your horse."

LeRoy gulped his whiskey and shuddered. "You ain't insinuating," he wheezed, pouring a second drink, "that mayhaps I fudged a tad?"

"Not a'tall. Horses are renowned as excellent rowboats."

"Damnit, it's plumb easier to handle frozen critters than live ones," LeRoy retorted, growing testy. "Live steers are right nasty when carried, liking to kick and bite and gouge with their horns. No sir, I'll take my frozen horse over your warm herd any day, Matt."

Crandon thumped his fist on the counter. "Enough. What now?"

"What now what?" Shelby asked, perplexed.

"Listen, we've been having a swell time swapping, uh, truths these last few days, but the woman's right. Enough's enough." Crandon eyed the others lined with him along the bar. "What'll we do now?"

Bishop shook his head. "I dunno. What do you want to do?"

Crandon shrugged, and Shelby looked even more baffled while he refreshed his glass. "I've done what I wanted to do. We're together."

"Oh, for gawdsake," LeRoy growled. "So we're together. So what? What we oughta do is be together back in Canta Lupe."

"Canta Lupe!" Shelby gasped, as Crandon and Bishop both reared, startled. "Guffy LeRoy, that's your biggest whopper to date!"

"What's wrong with my suggestion?" LeRoy demanded sternly, becoming very sincere about what had been an offhand notion. "We come from there, don't we? It wasn't a bad town. In fact, I remember it as having good booze, good eats, and good beds at the Social Club."

"The Social Club!" Bishop guffawed. "You're remembering the good broads there, Guffy, not the beds. Especially one, I betcha, that wild li'le filly you took such a shine to, Aurora Borealis."

"I am not! Well, even if I am a little, that ain't no different than you. You-all looked me up to find out how I've been faring. Why can't I be kinda curious about how a girl I once liked is faring?"

"You can, Guffy. You should," Crandon consoled, recalling his own lost love, his late wife Victoria. "It's just that . . . Well, I doubt Aurora will still be there, Guffy. A girl in her profession—"

"Whoa, Em," LeRoy warned. "She never charged me, not once."

Bishop grinned. "What'd you do, promise to marry her?"

"Matrimony," LeRoy assured him, "never entered my head. No sir, I'm strictly the moonlight-walk-and-dance-escort type of gent." Then, with a hint of maliciousness, he returned Bishop's jab. "But I imagine Heloise will be there and married, won't she, Matt?"

Bishop stiffened and, though it was a strain, managed to retain his grin. Crandon, standing beside him, craned and looked closer. "You're still not raw over her dumping you for Algernon's boy, are you?"

"Don't be silly. I couldn't care less," Bishop lied, and he knew the others knew he was lying. "Completely forgot her till this minute," he added, just as weakly. "I'm thinking of those huge steaks that were served at the Club. Hope it and they're still there."

"Then let's go find out," LeRoy urged.

"All we'll find out is how good the jail cells are," Shelby quavered. "We robbed the damn bank, Guffy! Have you forgotten that?"

"No, but I wager everyone else has."

"But if we're recognized . . ."

"Lord, Harold, you of all people worrying about that. How long did you say you lived in the same town with Tighe?" Crandon smiled, shaking his head. "I can't admit to be slavering at the gums to see Canta Lupe again, but Guffy's got a point. Tighe's dead, and the other lawmen who chased us way back then must've stepped outa their boots by now, too. Besides, even if we are recognized, we can't be arrested. The statute of limitations on our robbery expired years ago."

"Well, I suppose . . . If the rest of you want to, I suppose." Shelby mopped his brow. "We don't need to introduce ourselves, I guess."

LeRoy gave him the bottle. "Great. What about you, Matt?"

Bishop hesitated before answering, his thin face expressionless in the brief flare of a match as he lit one of his cheap cigars. Finally, in a cloud of noxious smoke, he replied, "Why not? I've got no reason to go, but I haven't got anything better to do."

"Then let's ride," LeRoy said airily. "Wait, no, I want to straighten out a little matter before we go. I'll be right back."

He hastened from the bar and returned in less than half an hour. "She's not mad at us anymore," he announced, thumbing in the direction of the cafe. "I signed over Hoffnagle's dig to her."

They killed the bottle before leaving and then, infused with a bleary glow, rode twenty miles that afternoon. And as Bishop lessened the distance between him and Canta Lupe, so grew the memories to crowd his mind. They pivoted around the clear, savage vision of Heloise Flynn. No, that was wrong; he had to quit thinking of her as Heloise Flynn, but instead as Mrs. Junius Algernon, the banker's daughter-in-law. Before Heloise was mostly a vague blur, punctuated by the deaths of his mother and then his father, a few agonies of the worst years, and fewer highlights of the nice ones. After Heloise was a blind urgency, a refusal to care much about anything, a need for rash action like the robbing of the bank, so that he'd be compelled to leave Canta Lupe forever.

He realized now, albeit dimly and without full comprehension, that these last twenty-five years were based on a fallacy; were guided by a self-deception inflicted by a young man's pain and disillusionment. Forever cannot exist, because time heals, time alters, time brings balance and maturity. That is, it's supposed to. Yet his decision to return to Canta Lupe had been just as swift and emotional as had been his one to leave. It was equally irrational, which didn't speak well of either time or himself. But that was the way it was. . . .

For nearly a month, the four old partners beat steadily south by southwest. Theirs was a rugged trail, pinched and folded into mountains and plains, forests and barren flats, and eroded wastelands. And it was a lonely trail, for beyond the occasional town or passing traveler, they were on their own in the seemingly endless wilderness. Eventually they reached southeastern Arizona, its terrain resembling a gray and tan blanket splattered with violet and burnt orange, and sweeping in an arid expanse toward purple-veiled mountains. And at last, near the end of yet another grueling day, they thought they could identify some familiar landmarks in the eroded contours ahead.

"Ain't that Dill Pickle mesa in front of us?" Shelby asked.

"If not, it's got a twin," Bishop allowed. "If we aim to pass just east of it and then angle south again, it seems to me that we'll run into Dimwiddy's old relay station on the Tucson-Las Cruces stage road."

LeRoy sighed fervently. "Maybe it's open and's got beer."

Encouraged, they moved on until they were on the other side of the mesa and had topped a shallow rise. They reined in, squinting, while their flagging horses nuzzled some dried yellow grass. First LeRoy and then the others stood in their stirrups, disbelieving the view.

"She-it!" LeRoy blurted. "What happened to Dimwiddy's?"

Crandon replied disgustedly, "Progress."

Beyond and below unraveled the ribbon of roadway, which had once been a major stagecoach route before the coming of trains. But instead of being in disrepair, the road appeared to've been widened and graded and even straightened in a number of places. Traffic was light yet consistent, mostly farm wagons and saddle horses, though interspersed with chugging automobiles and ungainly, chain-driven trucks.

Occasionally one of the vehicles would stop at Dimwiddy's, either pulling in by a large overhead tank painted with the legend, LAST CHANCE GAS in thick block letters, or parking over by the original ranch house and fenced corral which still stood as remembered. Now, however, the building's adobe walls gleamed a garish pink in the light of the westering sun; and along the corral fence were posted tall signs with fanciful illustrations and flamboyant copy like: THE ONE, THE ONLY, DESERT MUSEUM! LIVE DISPLAYS! SEE REAL HORN TOADS! SEE DEATH-STINGING SCORPIONS! SEE DEADLY SNAKES! SEE ANCIENT TREASURES OF OUR INDIAN HERITAGE!

In the corral and out around in the wide backyard, cages in various sizes and shapes had been arranged in haphazard rows. From the building's rear entrance would come people, usually families with sticky-fingered brats in tow, who'd meander along the aisles and sooner or later exit through the corral gate. A man sat under an umbrella by the gate, evidently there to make sure those who wanted in entered by paying an admission inside the house.

"Who'd want to pay money to see them things?" LeRoy asked, reading the signs. "Hell, they're all for free out here."

"Some folks are just passing through," Crandon tried to explain. "Some folks haven't the time to go look out here, to enjoy life."

"Enjoy?" Shelby stared appalled. "Scorpions? Snakes? Horny toads? *Enjoy* them? Hell, I only enjoy getting rid of the varmints!"

Bishop nodded. "I'd enjoy a beer, but I ain't stopping there."

"Yeah, I take back my wish. For gawdsake, let's give that crazy zoo a wide berth." Eyes rolling, LeRoy jiggered his horse moving again.

Crossing the highway and skirting Dimwiddy's Desert Museum, they veered toward the gentle incline of the Shadrack Hills. The sun continued its slow descent, burnishing the western slopes with slanting rays, and then extinguishing the fire with enveloping dusk. The shoulders of the hills began to loom against a dark velvet sky strewn with stars, and the riders knew that beyond those low, rolling shoulders lay the basin in which Canta Lupe was nestled.

They were within three to four hours of their destination. They could've continued across the Shadrack Hills, which were merely a series of broad undulations, like a corrugated plain—but it was riddled with cracks and crevices and leg-snapping burrow holes, and would be dangerous to navigate on a moonless night like this. They could also have backtracked to the highway, turned east and followed it to the intersection with the wagon road from Canta Lupe—but that was a fair piece, and would've used up much of the night to traverse. So instead they made camp at the foot of a treeless barranca, deciding to get a good sleep and an early start tomorrow.

Shelby, whose turn it was to be cook, was awake and foraging before dawn. The others were up, had breakfasted, and were cursing Shelby for fixing cannonball biscuits and eggs even a hen couldn't recognize, and were saddled and riding by the time first light struck the ridges.

Along about nine, they dropped out of the Shadrack Hills to the rim of the long oval basin. From here could be glimpsed Canta Lupe, already beginning to shimmer with heat, but the men avoided any mention of this as they headed toward its distant outline.

The only comment was from Crandon, as he glimpsed up at the warming sun. "It's going to be another scorcher of a day, I see."

Shelby nodded idly, and LeRoy gave an acknowledging tilt with his canteen before drawing a frugal sip, but that was all. They rode methodically, stoically, though inwardly they were tense and slightly apprehensive. The last time they'd been here had been when they'd ridden away—resulting in two and a half decades which had affected them profoundly, often unpleasantly. And now, by returning, they were forcing themselves to confess that however fast and far they'd ridden away, it had never been fast and far enough to exorcise the past and its ghosts. It was a troubling admission to make, and not one they wished to chat about.

CHAPTER 14

An hour later they arrived in Canta Lupe.

They sloped in from the north, trail-worn, neglected whiskers itching, clothes sweat-stained and dust-clogged; and they slowly walked their horses down Main Street while they scrutinized the town, feigning a lack of interest. Much was unchanged: the gnawed hitching rails, the warped boardwalks, the false-fronted feed store, cobbler, gunsmith, and barber shops. The same merchandise was stacked outside the EMPORIUM; and the bank looked as grim and unimpregnable as when they'd robbed it, with its stone block facade, oily, dark wood trim, and steel-barred windows.

The town had grown some, of course, adding a couple of cross streets, and a number of new businesses and saloons. The windows of a dressmaker and milliner displayed the latest fashions, and an upstart mercantile store had piled even more junk on its boardwalk to compete with the entrenched Emporium. There were more saloons, readily interchangeable with the already established barrooms.

More intriguing was how a few of the older places had altered. The ramshackle GENTEEL BOARDING HOUSE had been remodeled into a ritzy hotel and restaurant called EL VICTORIO. The original and fondly remembered SOCIAL CLUB brothel still stood at the northern edge of town, and for all they knew, still plied its trade; but it was all spruced up with fresh paint and curtains, and the sign under its porch overhang now read: NORTHERN LIGHTS, PURVEYORS OF FINE SPIRITS & FOOD & ENTERTAINMENT FOR THE DISCRIMINATING. The county sheriff's substation had expanded with a small wing on one side, but its office door was blocked open, as it'd always been, with a cast-off flatiron.

Leaning in the doorway and looking bored was a deputy sheriff, huskily built and about twenty-five, smoking a cigarette while surveying the passing scene with nonchalant eyes. The four riders could sense him giving them the once-over as they sauntered by, and though they didn't like it any more than anyone would, they weren't particularly worried. They could hardly get into trouble just by riding in, having a meal and a drink, and moving on in a day or so after their curiosity was satisfied. Besides, they appeared harmless, like overage saddle tramps riding the grub line, who at worst would be guilty of vagrancy.

Evidently the deputy thought so. He yawned.

They continued along Main Street, hock-deep in loose dust, until they reached the broad, squat livery stable at the south end. Leaving their horses with the hostler, they started walking back up the street, their saddlebags slung over their shoulders.

Crandon asked, "Where're we going?"

"For a beer," Shelby croaked.

LeRoy beamed. "At the Social Club."

"It's the Northern Lights now," Bishop corrected peevishly, "and that's all the way at the other side of town, Guffy!"

"Aw, c'mon, what's an extra five-minute walk?"

Grudgingly, they gave in to LeRoy's whim. "Twenty-five years, and he can't wait for us to have a beer," Crandon grumbled, and Shelby said thickly, "Hurry it up, then. I'm dehydrating on the spot."

The boardwalks weren't crowded, but they weren't deserted either, and in the swirl of people were a few faces that seemed vaguely familiar. The men were careful to return any glances with the briefest of nods, not slowing Shelby's thirst-driven pace as they hiked the length of Main Street toward the old brothel.

Midway, a tangle of traffic forced them to stop while a big freight outfit turned at the intersection and creaked ponderously up a cross street. Right behind the freighter crept a canvas-topped, green and black Hudson four-passenger open tourer. Its driver was a prig-faced youth in a Prussian-style chauffeur's uniform, who impatiently kept honking the car horn as if it were a goose call.

The freighter's teamster, maneuvering the corner, scowled back and loudly advised the driver to shove his horn where the sun don't shine. The driver, with a final honk, wheeled clear of the wagon's rear, accelerated up Main Street, and braked in front of the bank.

By then, the bank's old robbers had crossed the intersection. They were about a hundred feet away on the same side of the street, and couldn't miss seeing the Hudson's rear door open and the man step out. He had a lulu of a paunch, but otherwise was rather thin, and he was all gussied up in striped trousers, a Prince Albert coat, a paisley vest buttoned like a corset around his girth, and a tall plug hat.

LeRoy nudged Bishop. "Not that it means anything to you, Matt, but ain't we gazing at your sweetie's husband, Junius Algernon?"

Bishop bared his teeth. "That's Mister Algernon to you, Guffy."

"To all of us and everybody else," Shelby interjected, chuckling. "A prosperous banker's gotta act the part, as well as look it, eh?"

Junius Algernon took off his plug hat and pompously flicked off a spot of dust, while a second passenger slid across and joined him. It was the one person Matt Bishop yearned to avoid: Heloise.

"Damned if she don't look like a million bucks too, Matt," Crandon said, pausing beside Bishop, who'd come to an abrupt halt with his features set rigid as though chiseled in marble.

Algernon started in talking to her—or, rather, talking at her—clapping his hat back on, and then reeling out a gold watch the size of a turnip. He kept gesturing with it like a pointer while he talked.

Heloise stood listening, so stylishly and properly clad that it was difficult for Bishop to judge how the years had been treating her. She was swaddled in a modest suit of powder blue Venetian wool cloth, tailored full-length and close-throated, and trimmed with velvet and satin of royal blue. Her Italian leghorn hat hid the coils of her rich auburn hair, which Bishop recalled flowing freely in the wind as she rode; and the hat's wide-swept brim shadowed her face, which Bishop in his poetic adolescence had once considered to be pixieish.

Yet from what little he could discern, the passage of time had been kind. Her figure was still trim and shapely, and she still stood tall, almost regally erect. And when she moved, as suddenly she did, he perceived she still possessed her lithe, fluid grace.

Turning, Heloise ducked partially into the Hudson's rear compartment, and began to awkwardly unload a series of boxes, the kind clothes are sent home from the store in. Algernon didn't help her or even volunteer the chauffeur; he just continued on spouting, thrusting his watch about and tapping his forefinger against its crystal.

After removing six boxes and stacking them on the boardwalk, Heloise shut the car door, then hesitated for a moment, averting her face as though weary of being badgered. In that moment, in that chance twist of her head, she stared directly at Bishop. Her hazel eyes widened and her full lips parted breathlessly, but Bishop doubted it was because she happened to recognize him. No, it was on account of Algernon having gripped her unexpectedly during that same moment, shaking her as he clutched her arm and forced her to face him again. She nodded demurely, once more attentive to her husband's lecture.

"Hey, we can't root here, y'know," Crandon said.

Bishop swiveled around. "Then let's go back."

"But I want to hit the Social Club," LeRoy complained.

"Guffy, tween it and us is the only person who can cause us any serious trouble. We can go there later, when he's not here."

"We heisted Ichabod Algernon, not his son," Crandon said.

"Yeah, only Junius 'pears the spitting image of his ol' man. Lard-brained and petty, and sneaky-nasty when riled. No telling what he might pull, and no sense risking finding out," Shelby argued, then shrugged. "Don't matter, though. He's leaving."

Pivoting frontward again, Bishop saw that, indeed, Junius Algernon was now striding toward the bank entrance, wedging his gold watch back into his vest pocket. The Hudson was easing away up the street again. Only Heloise remained, standing with her boxes.

"Let's go," LeRoy said cheerily and winked at Bishop. "Don't fret if we rub elbows passing Heloise, Matt. She's contented wallowing in her wealth, and never'll see you. She can't."

Irked by LeRoy's joshing and irritated at himself for letting it nettle him, Bishop forged up the boardwalk. Heloise had her back to them, but just as a precaution Bishop tucked his head down and lowered his hat brim. Nearing, he began to feel that his strange reluctance was all in his mind and that getting by her would be a waltz. Then Shelby jabbed an elbow in his ribs.

"Christ, the law is coming our way."

Looking ahead, Bishop saw the deputy sheriff strolling casually along, twirling his stick. "He's just making his rounds. Don't panic."

Instead, Bishop panicked when, without warning, Heloise shifted around and glanced at them. She crooked a finger in Bishop's general direction. "You, there. I need your assistance."

Bishop's throat tightened. "Not us, ma'am, sorry."

"I most certainly do mean you!" Heloise said sharply, now pointing her finger. "I can't carry all these boxes by myself."

They didn't respond, hoping to hasten past without further ado, only to be confronted by the approaching deputy, who was no longer casual about the way he held his stick. "Problem, Mrs. Algernon?"

"Thank you, Max, but I don't believe so. I was hoping these

gentlemen would help take my dresses here to the seamstress for me."

The deputy put his hands on his hips and regarded the four. "And just what do you *gentlemen* have to say to this fine lady?"

Crandon coughed apologetically. "We're in a hurry, y'see—"

The deputy interrupted by poking his stick into Crandon's belly. "You're in a hurry, alright, to do exactly what Mrs. Algernon bids o' you. Or I'll be in a hurry to learn if gentlemen can also be bums."

Shelby, in somewhat of a fit, snatched Bishop's saddlebags off his shoulder and bleated, "You take her boxes. I'll hold your bags."

"Wait—"

"And mind you don't drop them," Heloise ordered, picking up the top box on the stack and handing it to Bishop. Then she proceeded to pile on three more, and would've added the last two, if Crandon hadn't quickly given LeRoy his saddlebags and taken them himself.

The deputy grunted approvingly. "Now, if any o' these buckoes so much as breathes wrong, ma'am, you tell me and I'll put a stop to it."

"I'm sure I won't find fault with them now, thanks to you, Max," Heloise purred, then swung haughtily back to the men. "Follow me."

They tagged after, while she traipsed blithely across the street, seemingly oblivious to the snarled wagon teams and bolting saddle horses she left in her wake, or to the four men who dodged, staggering under their cumbersome loads of bags and boxes. Then down the other boardwalk she sailed, until she came to the dressmaker's shop, where she waited for one of the men to fumble the door open for her.

Inside, she directed Bishop and Crandon to set her boxes on a long, low worktable. "There'll be two dresses for delivery at two-thirty," she said crisply, and turned to the seamstress. "Right?"

The stooped old woman shivered. "Yes'm, yes'm."

Bishop gritted his teeth. "Hold on, ma'am, we can't all—"

"Heavens, no! I fully expect you alone can carry both boxes, and to be on time." She cast him a severe look. "I'm positive you can, if you put your mind to it. Do you know where my house is?"

Bishop knew, but he didn't dare admit it. He also had the violent urge to ask if it wasn't one of the dog-pound kennels, but he managed to control his temper and reply curtly, "I'll find out from helpful Max."

"A clever idea." She unclasped her chatelaine purse and gave a quarter each to Bishop and Crandon. "Don't thank me, gentlemen. I always like to be generous for services rendered, especially to those who look deserving," she said, shooing them to the door, where she paused for a last withering fix on Bishop. "Two-thirty promptly. And I trust your friends will see you don't spend it all on alcohol."

The door shut with a rattle, leaving the men gawking.

"So that's how li'le Heloise growed up," Crandon said in awe, as they slowly trudged up the boardwalk again. "I reckon it's a blessing, ol' Jenny Flynn dyin' before she discovered what she'd foaled."

LeRoy, having tossed Crandon back his saddlebags, used his free hand to pat Bishop comfortingly on the arm. "Matt, we've ragged each other about our old flames, but we were only joking. But in all seriousness, I've gotta tell you, a man's better off being a bank robber caught in prison, than a bank owner married to that hellion."

"A-men," Shelby intoned. "Why, I'd actually choose Cornelia over her, and that's no trifle. You've got more balls'n me, I don't mind admitting, Matt, to be braving to go see her in her own lair."

"Hell, no! Somebody else can go!"

"Y'think she's queening it up in the Algernon mansion?" LeRoy asked, and then answered himself. "She must be. Ichabod was at least seven zillion years old when we left, and

Junius wouldn't be strutting so cocky if he weren't chief honcho now. Rumored to be a right fancy hen coop, not that us common folk ever got to peek inside. You keep a sharp eye so you can tell us how grand it is, will you?"

"Are you mad?" Bishop yelled. "I ain't stepping near it!"

"Sure you are, with them boxes later on this afternoon," Crandon reminded him. "If you don't, that deputy will fry our hides."

"That's your lookout! Me, I'm skedaddling, and this time I'm going to stay skedaddled!" A tinge of frenzy laced Bishop's voice. "Why am I even heading this way? The livery's back the other way!"

Shelby sighed. "Well, I guess we'd all better go, then."

"Not yet," LeRoy pleaded. "We ain't visited the Social Club."

"The Northern Lights," Crandon insisted. "Get it right, Guffy."

"Whatever the damn name is, we've got time to drop in! Matt doesn't hafta show until two-thirty, so what's all the rush to leave?"

"None, really," Bishop agreed, nodding morosely. "I don't want to break up your fun, Guffy, and besides, I'm in sore need of a drink."

They continued along the noon-simmering street to the Northern Lights, which was a three-story, peaked-roof house, if not precisely a home, built of clapboard rather than the usual adobe. Its hitching rail was lined with drowsing horses, and Shelby noted as they trooped to the door, "For it being daylight, the place seems plumb popular."

"Luncheon trade," Crandon suggested.

"Or maybe it's gone respectable," LeRoy said anxiously.

Inside was dim and cool, shielded from the sun's glare and heat by heavy, floor-length window drapes. The men hesitated, blinded until their eyes had adjusted, and then they crossed a short, square foyer. On both sides were wide archways, the one on the right connecting to a dining hall, and the one on the left to a barroom. At the rear was a counter desk, behind which sat an elderly man with a beet-red face, and next to it was a curving staircase leading to the upper floors.

The foyer's ceiling shook as something thumped to the floor above, and a woman's laugh echoed down the steps. "No, it's just like it always was," LeRoy declared, brightening, drifting toward the stairs.

"A beer, Guffy," Bishop said, snagging him by the arm. "Maybe two, but that's all. Nice 'n' peaceable, no fancy notions, that's our deal."

"Yeah, 'cept—"

"Guffy, she ain't up there," Crandon cut in and took his other arm to help Bishop propel him into the barroom. "I don't care how talented she was, she can't still be at it, not after twenty-five years."

"Lemme know if you change your minds, or if something else pops up of interest," the man at the desk called after and cackled.

The crowded, low-ceilinged barroom was even darker than the foyer, only one lantern in the center shedding a pallid, smoky glow. The men settled at a table near the archway, in a corner next to one of the draped front windows; and, when a bucktoothed girl in a sequined, hourglass costume came by, they ordered a pitcher of beer and four mugs.

For a while they talked wistfully of old times spent drinking here before sporting upstairs. Another hostess carrying a bowlfull of fresh eggs paused to ask if they wanted an egg for their beer, and it was then that LeRoy demanded, "Alright, which one of you jokers is tryin' to play footsy with my bum leg?"

Nobody knew what he was talking about, so they checked under the table. A hefty, yellow-striped tomcat was rubbing up against LeRoy's metal shin, having for some unknown reason taken a shine to it.

"That's Tiger, our house pet," the egg girl explained. "I'm sorry, he must've entered through the window there behind you.

We keep it ajar for him to come 'n' go as he likes. I'll get rid of him."

"Naw, he's okay. Bring him some milk, why don'cha?"

LeRoy's kindness toward the pussycat called for a second pitcher. They talked some more of nothing in particular, and the cat had about finished its saucer of milk, when Bishop felt someone standing close by.

His chair was nearest the foyer, and, turning, Bishop saw a tall, beefy man in range garb leaning against the archway. The man's gaze skimmed over Bishop and the others, then continued to survey the barroom as though searching for someone in particular. Then grunting with satisfaction, the man stepped back into the foyer, where Bishop could glimpse him checking the Seth Thomas wall clock behind the counter.

"What's the matter?" Shelby asked.

Bishop shrugged. "Nothin'. Just a guy acting like he's looking for somebody, but not wanting to find him till the right time, is all."

"That's the stupidest answer I've ever heard tell," Crandon began, only to be interrupted by the man staggering into the barroom and bumping into Bishop's chair. Bishop was sent lurching into the table, almost upsetting the pitcher, while the man steadied himself and bawled drunkenly, "Anyone seen that goddamn Thorpe?"

A hush spread over the barroom.

"Thorpe came in here, I know he did!" The man stumbled forward a few more steps and brushed his hand across his mouth. "Awri', you yaller sonofabitch, show yourself, I know you're in here a-hidin'!"

"Funny," Bishop muttered, "how he got boiled so fast."

LeRoy perked attentively. "You don't suppose . . ."

"Hey, you!" The man lunged in an ungainly way toward the bar at the far side of the room. From the row of drinkers bellied there, another man turned to give him a quick glare and then turned back to his glass. This second man was a good inch taller than the first, and heavier in the shoulders and chest.

That didn't seem to daunt the man, who grabbed the drinker and whirled him harshly around to face him.

"For the las' time, Thorpe, you stop pesterin' my wife!"

"Then you'd best tell her to stop sucking after me, Wylie!"

"Cut it out, you two," the bartender warned, a fleshy man with jowls and a shiny scalp. He leaned across the bar. "No fighting here."

The man named Wylie put his palm into the bartender's face and shoved. The bartender careened into the backbar, dumping bottles and glasses as, with a swipe of his hand, he tumbled to the plank floor.

And LeRoy stood up. "It is! They're running a whipsaw play," he growled indignantly. "They're planning to bust up the place!"

"I'll blow your head off!" Wylie was shouting at Thorpe, ignoring the bartender as his hand dropped to his holstered revolver.

"Don't draw on me!" Thorpe snarled, grabbing Wylie's shirt, while Wylie raised an old .45 Colt and wavered it at the bar mirror.

"Not in *my* place, they can't!" LeRoy fumed and, before the others could haul him back into his seat, he pitched his heavy mug.

Wylie howled as the beer mug bounced off his head. He reeled from Thorpe's dubious grip, his Colt slamming loads aimlessly into the floor in front of him, while the mug ricocheted in a short arc and banished behind the bar counter, and the customers and hostesses started scrambling wildly for cover.

"Peaceable, Guffy!" Bishop snapped, as he and Crandon sprang from their chairs. "Damnation, you swore we'd keep it peaceable!"

All four knew from experience what was coming. Wylie was dazed but not down, and with Thorpe backing his play, would be enraged and eager to turn on them as his excuse to wreck the barroom. LeRoy was too slow because of his false leg, and Shelby was momentarily stuck in the corner by the window, so it was up to Bishop and Crandon to move in fast and stop the two men before matters got any worse.

Bishop, in the lead, attacked Wylie first. He just kept his two long arms windmilling, pummeling face, chest, and gut to detract Wylie from firing his revolver again. Crandon was delayed by the egg girl, who almost dumped into him with her bowl as she ran hysterically around in squirrel-like fits and starts. This probably saved Crandon's life as well, for by now Thorpe had yanked his S&W .44 from the waistband of his pants and was leveling it, squeezing its trigger. Crandon, ducking the egg girl, felt the powder burn of Thorpe's first shot. Crandon dove before Thorpe could correct his aim, and the egg girl went shrieking into another erratic dance.

Meanwhile, Shelby had upended the table in his frenzy to get out from his corner. The remaining three mugs crashed with it, but LeRoy had managed to snatch up the pitcher an instant before it toppled. Yelling, " 'Tain't my fault!" he reared back to throw the pitcher.

His windup was good, but when he shifted his weight forward–as one must when tossing hard–LeRoy accidentally caught his metal foot on the lip of the milk saucer and twisted his ankle socket. There was a twang of twangers, and his leg suddenly kicked high, launching the tomcat, which had been trying to purr against his leg in a friendly manner, clean to the low ceiling.

Thrown off-balance, the pitcher missed Wylie but struck Thorpe on his shoulder. Beer cascaded over him, his second bullet tunneling up through the ceiling into the bedroom above. A muffled scream and some startled cursing could be heard, but these sounds were swiftly drowned by Crandon charging into Thorpe and knocking him soundly against the bar.

One of the more courageous customers leaped to the rescue, only to run into Bishop's solid, bony fist as it glanced off Wylie's chin. The punch tipped the customer back into two other men, and together they caromed sprawling into the wreckage of a table. Infuriated, one of the other two men took a swipe at the customer, and this pretty much was the signal for all the men in the barroom to join in the fray.

The cat, by now, had descended. Spitting like a trapped lynx, it made a desperate bound for the open window, landing first on Shelby, who'd been crawling free around the edge of the table, digging claws into the bald spot on his head and then slashing past the drapes and out.

Shelby's squawk of pain mingled with the protesting whinnies abruptly arising from the front yard, as the startled feline dashed across the rumps of the horses. The saddled mounts belonging to Thorpe and Wylie were not tied to the hitching rail, but had purposely been left ground-reined in case their owners had to beat a hasty retreat. Spooking, they tore around the side and came up against the fence at the rear of the building, and, still frantic to escape, wheeled and bolted in through the open kitchen door.

The fat cook and two hostesses fled out into the barroom, chased by the two horses breathing fire right behind them. The egg girl, who'd almost reached what she'd assumed was the safety of the kitchen, was thrown into a somersault. Her bowl upended onto the cook, knocking her flat and drenching her with eggs, while the horses galloped past and through the archway, into the foyer and dining hall.

Angrier than a boiled owl, the cook scooped up a handful of busted eggs, clapped a hand on the back of the egg girl's head, and screwed that omelet into her face. Apparently a hostess was friends with the egg girl, for, taking offense, she tackled the cook and began yanking hair. The other hostess, having slipped on the eggs and sat down, flung the bowl and then everything else within reach.

Simultaneously, Bishop was still trying to overcome Wylie. Grappling Wylie's gun wrist and wrenching down viciously, he forced Wylie to hinge forward, and for a moment their strained faces were mere inches apart. Peripherally Bishop realized the extent of the storm raging in the barroom. Men and women were tangling amid the kindling of tables and chairs, while glassware and spittoons and sundry other deadly weapons were flying through the air, and the horses were returning via the kitchen again, the few folk who'd been eating in the dining hall in full rout before them.

Then Bishop jabbed a knee into Wylie's groin and let go. Wylie slumped kneeling, gagging, cupping his crotch as he slowly tipped forward, until his head touched the floor in a prayerlike position.

Crandon had Thorpe by the neck and was half throttling him while he bashed his head against the bar. The counter splintered loose from its floor brace and tilted over, Thorpe tumbling with it. Before Thorpe could recover and scuttle free from the debris behind the bar, Crandon stepped in to kick Thorpe in the face. His boot struck Wylie's temple, just as Wylie managed to trigger a third time.

The .44 slug whined by Crandon and punctured the hanging lamp. The flame snuffed out, plunging the barroom into a pitch-black typhoon of rocketing articles, painful yelps and hysterical squeals, and trampling hoofs as the horses hit the foyer and charged up the stairs. Abruptly from above came a panicky racket of women and the discriminating men they were entertaining, but it was barely heard over the barroom roar.

Hastily, Bishop began moving in a crouch. A hand touched his arm, and he whispered sharply, "Is that you, Em?"

"I think so," Crandon hissed nervously. "But I kinda wish it wasn't, and I was someplace a long ways away from where I am."

"C'mon, let's get back to the table, anyway."

Warily, but swiftly, they groped through the dark tumult, and located Shelby and LeRoy hunching behind the overturned table.

LeRoy rose to give warning. "Hurry, take cover!" And as if to emphasize the need, he was immediately beaned by a slab of bacon. "Greatgawdalmighty, them gals will kill all us men yet!"

Bishop and Crandon slid in, making themselves as small as

possible as the insane tomcat crawled in from the window and scampered past.

"I've never seen such a howling massacre," Shelby moaned. He opened his mouth to say more, but was interrupted by a male voice yowling from somewhere beyond the table. "M'beard! Somethin's clawin' my beard! Holy Moses, there's a cougar loose in here!"

The din in the barroom increased, the people upstairs surging downstairs in various states of undress. The horses arrived too, one with a portion of sheet snagged to its saddle horn; but instead of touring another circuit of the ground floor, they hit the window at the back of the barroom neck-and-neck. Glass and clapboard siding erupted in fragments, the horses ramming right through the wall of the old, weatherworn house, dragging the window casement along and flattening a section of the rear fence as they stampeded out of sight.

The sudden blast of sunlight put an instant dampener on the riot. Men and women began to unravel themselves from the ruins, fingering swelling eyes and wiggly teeth. The egg girl had been shorn of her hourglass costume, and was sitting naked on the floor, bawling like a child. One of the men was stumbling around seeking an unbroken bottle; there was blood in his bristly beard, and it streaked his grizzled chin. Wylie and Thorpe lay blissfully unconscious. Lots of running boots could be heard approaching from the street outside.

"Peaceful!" Bishop raged at LeRoy. "Quiet 'n' peaceful, that's all we had to be! Now just look at the fine mess you got us in!"

"Tell me about it later, Matt. Now let's get the hell outa here." LeRoy straightened, only to fall back behind the table again. The men who'd come up from the street stopped just outside the archway.

"What's going on in here?" a familiar voice shouted, and Deputy Max poked his head in. "Sufferin' snakes, it ain't possible!"

"What isn't?" a husky woman's voice asked behind him.

Without turning, Max told her, "Best not come in, ma'am."

Wearily she said, "I've seen it all, Deputy, and probably worse," and entered the barroom. She was a formidable-breasted, henna-haired woman, her features round, almost moon-like, and not unpleasant. She was buttressed and cinched in a voluminous dark silk dress, and appeared less a stout matron than a plump grandma, who should be baking pies for church socials instead of surveying the shambles of a whorehouse barroom. "I retract that, Max," she said, marveling at the sight. "No, I've never seen anything worse'n this."

And Max, glimpsing the four men behind the table, stomped over and stared at them, his expression gnarled with fury. "You again!"

Bishop stiffened, but Shelby said hesitantly, "Now . . . now we can explain, Deputy. We didn't come in here looking for no trouble, honest."

"No, but I'll wager a month's wages you're the cause of it!"

The woman turned and regarded the men, but they couldn't tell if it was with disgust or admiration. Yet something else, something deeper and more innate, seemed to strike a spark in LeRoy as he looked back at her, for apprehensively, almost meekly, he asked, "Aurora?"

"Why, yes, how did you . . ." She paused, tilting her head to stare at LeRoy, a flicker of uncertainty in her gaze. "No, you're not . . ."

"That's right, lambikins!"

"Oh, my stars and garters! Guffy, you ol' rapscallion!"

The deputy's train of thought continued rolling along its own narrow track. "Border ruffians, ma'am, I know the sort. I've already had one run-in with them today, and I'll take 'em in—"

"Not on your life," Aurora cut in, a gleam to her eye and her tone brooking no argument. "You just go about your business, Max, and I'll tend to mine. And these fellows are definitely my business!"

The deputy was floored, disbelieving his ears.

And Bishop, Shelby, and Crandon blinked at one another, and then eyeballed the fatuously grinning LeRoy. *"Lambikins?"* they chorused.

CHAPTER 15

"Your red hair's white, and you look like you've gone from thin to fat to thin again without pausing in between," Aurora said, leading the way up the stairs. "But your grin hasn't changed a whit, Guffy. By drat, I could pick that grin out among a thousand."

"Well, it got mislaid awhile," he replied, thinking of how sour he'd been before being rescued from Captain Eloise's hideout. "Near lost my humor and my head permanently, and that's a fact."

Along the second-floor corridor, a mattress canted half out of one room, a door dangled on twisted hinges, and a pile of manure steamed on the runner rug, but otherwise there didn't appear to be too much damage from the horses. Aurora ushered the men into her private parlor, whose decor was fancy in an overstuffed manner, even to having curlicue designs on the glass of the lamps.

She ensconced LeRoy on a tufted, plush sofa, sinking beside him while the others settled around in fringed armchairs. "It's wonderful, seeing you-all boys again," she said with genuine warmth. "You bring back a lot of fun memories, back when we were . . . Well, you know."

"You still are," LeRoy responded in a rare burst of gallantry, but it fizzled out when he tried to embellish it. "Why, you're lovely as . . . That is, you're still the same as . . . I mean, you are, aren't you?"

"Stop babbling, Guffy, I'm certainly not. I'm twice the girl I was, both outside, where I wish I wasn't, and inside, where it counts. Here." She thumped her whalebone-stayed bosom, and for a moment the men feared a rupturing that would catapult even more of her outside. "But what on earth brought you back to Canta Lupe?" she asked, leaning to look at LeRoy. "My heavens, you've got grease on your face."

She whipped a handkerchief from her dress sleeve and began scrubbing LeRoy's face. "What brought this about?" she asked.

LeRoy, squirming, evaded her handkerchief long enough to answer, "It was all your dad-ratted females' faults. They were throwing a regular breakfast down there, eggs and pork whizzing every which way, shrieking and pulling hair and ripping clothes. I tell you, Aurora, gents are right gentlefolk compared to those ladies you've got here."

"I don't mean the bacon, I mean the reason you're here."

The other three came to LeRoy's aid, launching into a short and carefully edited version of the events leading to their arrival.

"So you see, Aurora," Crandon finished, "we only dropped in here for old times' sake, and had no idea we'd get involved in a brawl."

Shelby nodded. "Or that the place is yours. I feel terrible about what happened. I don't know what we can do to make it up to you."

"Forget it. There's been a war going on around here awhile, and you're merely the latest battle." Aurora stuffed her handkerchief away and sighed tremulously. "The last battle, I daresay."

"Oh? Why the fight?"

"Same old story, Matt. Them that have want more, and them that haven't want some." She smiled thinly. "Listen, when'd you eat last?"

"A decent meal? So long ago I can't remember," LeRoy said, pushing a hand tiredly across his clean face. "But if you're offering, don't. I think the horses pretty well demolished your kitchen, too."

"Nonsense. Food's my main activity these days, and I simply

won't tolerate excuses about it." Standing, Aurora went to the door and bellowed down the corridor, "Enough for five, make it snappy!"

When she wheeled to return to the sofa, she caught sight of LeRoy's left leg and gasped in shock. "M'Lord, Guffy! Your foot!"

"Eh?"

"Your foot! It's pointing backward!"

Grimacing, LeRoy leaned down and swiveled his leg around. "The ankle's out of whack," he grumbled embarrassedly. "Whole leg is metal, Aurora, but it's the best there's to get. Weren't cheap."

"Oh, if that's all it is . . ." She slumped to the sofa, fanning herself. "I hope the rest of you is real. You don't have a tin–"

"Just m'leg!" LeRoy responded hastily, and Bishop laughed. "You're still full of the devil, Aurora. No, you haven't changed."

"How could I, Matt? Where else could a girl in my trade go? What else could she do? Who'd want one for a wife and mother?" She paused, glimpsing LeRoy, who, already blushing, was now turning deep crimson. Rouge had given life to her cheeks and lips, but the twinkle in her eyes was genuine as she smiled at him. "Thanks, Guffy, that's sweet of you," she said gently, then turned to Bishop again. "No, I saved my money, and when Mrs. Teagarden wanted to retire, I bought the Social Club from her. Fixed it up and renamed it–Northern Lights kinda goes with Aurora Borealis, don't you think?–and I've had my ups and downs, mostly ups. Just now it's down, and likely for good."

Shelby said, "Twice you've mentioned this. Tell us, why?"

"In a nutshell, Junius Algernon is out to close me."

Crandon frowned. "What'n hell for? Is he on a moral crusade?"

"Worse'n that. He wants to take the house over."

"Y'mean, and run it?" It was LeRoy's turn to laugh, and he

laughed till he got the hiccups. "An' Heloise as the madam? Gawd!"

"She might do alright," Aurora mused, somewhat soberly. "Junius was doing okay as a silent partner operating El Victorio, but he lacks the contacts and, ah, experience I have. It was the best around until I opened, and then it was only natural that I'd attract a lot of his trade away. He's been waylaying for me ever since."

A knock sounded, and the hostesses entered, bearing food and drink. Serving, they stared curiously at the four grubby men they recalled from the barroom, while the men nodded appreciatively, first at the girls and then at the plates mountained with meat, potatoes, bread, and vegetables. The hostesses left extra helpings and bottles on a sideboard, gracefully exited, and closed the door after them.

For a while, talk was suspended in favor of eating, the savory meal lifting the men's spirits and dissipating their fatigue and tension. Finally Bishop, swabbing his plate clean with a crust of bread, said to Aurora, "I'm glad to hear somebody's gotten Junius to squeal like a stuck pig. You must've been hurting him powerful hard in the wallet."

Aurora smiled sardonically. "Hardly. His bank vault is so squeezed with dinero that it bulges like a Texas sausage. No, he simply can't stand taking second place, not even in bordellos."

"What's he been doing to you?" Crandon asked.

"First he tried to buy me out. His offers weren't high, but they weren't low either. And it's not that I'm set against selling; this's a business I know, not one I particularly like. I just don't want to sell to him is all, and I don't care what price he quotes." Aurora took another dainty bite, then put her fork aside. "Anyway, when Junius realized he couldn't dicker with me, he bought up my mortgage loan I'd floated at a Tucson bank. You can believe the instant I fall short or overdue, Junius'll foreclose and assume the note."

"He's still stymied," Shelby said. "You're making plenty."

"I would be, if it wasn't for all the fights and hooliganism that've been wrecking things, injuring my girls and rousting my customers."

"Yeah, like the whipsaw play we stopped," LeRoy declared. "Well, that we kinda helped, I guess, actually. But yeah, I wouldn't put it past Junius to've hired those pugs and whatever else, too."

"I've my suspicions, but no proof." Aurora shook her head. "I've had to spend my payment money for repairs and doctor bills, and for hiring extra bouncers. If I don't, I'm good as closed anyway."

Shelby rubbed his jaw. "Suppose if . . ."

"What, Harold?" Crandon asked.

Shelby shrugged. "Nothing. How much do you owe, Aurora?"

"Three thousand, by the end of this week."

"And we ain't got a dime," LeRoy groaned.

"Too bad," Shelby murmured, still stroking his jaw. "A dime would buy a shave, leastwise, and I'm sure in need of one."

Crandon, exasperated, snapped, "Well, if it bothers you so much, borrow a razor and go down and shave at the horse trough."

"Fine, and I'll make room for you to take a bath in it," Shelby retorted good-naturedly. "Here we are, visiting a fine lady and a fond acquaintance, and we're all stinking and scratchy foul."

LeRoy sniffed tentatively, caught his own ripe aroma, and looked apologetically at Aurora. "Hell, a dunkin' wouldn't hurt us none."

Aurora chuckled. "Alright, boys, the treat's on me, if you promise to return. Tell the barber to put the works on my tab."

"We'll be back." Bishop stood, smiling with more assurance than he felt. "And don't worry, we'll figure a way out for you."

"There isn't a way, Matt, and we all know it."

"That's no reason for us not to try. . . ."

The four went downstairs, where Aurora's girls, desk clerk, and a few volunteer customers were trying to straighten the shambles. Outside and heading down the boardwalk toward the nearest barber, Crandon suddenly turned on LeRoy and demanded, "Whaddyuh mean, we ain't got a dime? We've still got a little money left over from our trip here; not much, but damn well enough to pay for our own cleaning!"

"It wasn't meant exactly, only compared to three grand!"

"You can't fool us," Bishop taunted. "You were just trying to weasel another kind of free treat outa her. Is that how you used to get it free in the old days, Guffy? By pleading poor?"

"You dumb lunkhead!" LeRoy yelled. "Is you so ignorant that you never heard tell of an expression of speech? I, uh . . ." His voice suddenly dropped to a whisper. "Why, hello there, Depitty Max."

The deputy had seemingly sprung out of nowhere, as though he'd been lurking in hiding expressly for them. "I want you no-account drifters off my streets and outa my town by sundown." His palm caressed the butt of his pistol. "Else I'll carry you out."

"But there's Mrs. Algernon, and Miz Borealis–"

"Out." The deputy's voice hardened. "By sundown."

"Yes, y'honor," Shelby quickly agreed, and kicked Crandon in the shin to keep him from any more arguing. "G'day to you, yessir."

They hastened along the boardwalk, feeling the deputy's eyes burning into their spines, and ducked into the barber shop. The barber, a dyspeptic man with a clipped moustache and the smudge of a little goatee, looked up and said, "If you want all that there shrubbery of yours hacked off, I'll have to use pruning shears and charge you double."

"Go to it," LeRoy responded, settling into the chair. "An' baths for us afterward. You're looking at your new town council."

The barber complained and fretted as he mowed his way through each of the four, sending them shorn and shaven into the back room where they wallowed in large wooden tubs of hot water.

Soaking, Bishop twirled his now neatly trimmed moustache, and worried that too much had been cut off. "Feel plumb naked, I do."

"Like Samson, eh?" Shelby said from his tub. "Reckon we all do, naked and vun'rable, us and Aurora. Downright defenseless."

LeRoy gave a snort. "Junius sure ain't, not with his bloat. I bet he thinks it gives him a certain air of authority, but far's I'm concerned, I'd like to stick a pin in and let it leak out."

"I wouldn't mind pounding some respect into him, either," Bishop said, sliding lower, his back and shoulder muscles aching the way they usually did in rainy, cold weather. He flexed to ease the cramping pain and added, "Yeah, or if nothing else, break him of his hassling Aurora. I could leave town happy then, knowing Aurora's okay."

The barber and Aurora's desk clerk came in from the front and dumped four sets of new underwear, socks, Levi's, and flannel shirts on the plank flooring. "Compliments of the Northern Lights," the clerk said and began emptying out and wadding their old clothes.

"Great," LeRoy said. "You goin' to wash ours now?"

"My instructions are to burn 'em," the clerk replied.

Crandon watched the clerk and barber, and, when at last they'd left, he turned speculative eyes on Shelby. "Okay, Harold, you've been more'r less silent for too long a time, and I know you well enough to know that wheels and cogs are movin' in your head. So how about it? What were you supposin' back up there at Aurora's?"

Shelby nodded. "Watch the door," he said and then in a hushed tone he began, "Suppose— Just suppose, we rob the bank."

"You're nuts!" LeRoy blurted, and Bishop's reaction was hardly less flattering. Crandon shushed them both, saying, "Listen, Harold dreamt up our original heist, so maybe he's onto something again."

Shelby paused for attention, then continued, "I'm not much

for planning—you were always best there, Emmett—but I do see that beating Junius to a pulp has to fail. He'd only mend and be just as powerful, just as much an ass, while we'd be on the lam, unable to save Aurora and likely ourselves from his vengeful spite. No, our only hope to win is to deflate him, like Guffy suggested; to strip him defenseless and leave him more naked and vunerable than we are now."

"C'mon, Harold, all that from a bank heist?"

"Remember your words up at Aurora's, Matt? You said she must've been hurting him hard in his wallet. True! Take his money, we've taken his power and punctured his air of importance that owning a rich bank's swollen him with. And Aurora said he hated taking second place. Well, take his money and he'd be no place, a nobody."

LeRoy chuckled. "It'd sting him, it'd really sting Junius to be ripped like his ol' man was, but . . . Hell, Harold, this ain't twenty-five years ago. Then, it was a snap. We cased the bank for a few days to learn the routines, then walked in at closing time, waved our guns around, got our gunnysacks filled, and rode hell-and-gone for leather."

"I'm not denying it. The bank had no electricity, only a rheumatic guard and a hand-cranked siren, and the closest we came to dyin' was when Ichabod Algernon pooped in his pants from fright. And I'm not insisting it can be done again now. My point is that, possible or not, it's the only way, and we can forget about the rest."

"We can forget about *it,* too," Bishop growled.

"Interesting, though. . . . Electric alarms now, telephones, maybe time locks . . ." Crandon's mind wandered off, his eyes looking as murky as his bathwater. "Obviously, the key is how much the bank's security has changed," he said finally. "The trick'll be to find out now, this afternoon, 'cause we've only till sundown to hit the bank."

Bishop remained skeptical. "That info is kept secret, Em. Nobody knowing it'll tell us about it, not in the hours we've got."

Crandon grinned blandly. "Heloise might."

"I won't!" Bishop paled. "I can't!"

"Try," Shelby pleaded. "Go and deliver her boxes and try to persuade her to confide in you. If it doesn't work, okay, it doesn't and we forget it and no harm done. But she's our only source."

"I'd rather romance a polecat!"

"You promised Aurora, Matt!" LeRoy hooted, laughing so hard he almost upset his tub. "Well, we've figured a way to help, right?"

"Shut up, you!" Bishop stood, fists clenched. "Besides, us looting the bank won't get Junius to lay off Aurora, it won't!"

"It will," Crandon argued. "We cut her a share. Junius'll never be able to link her payments with his stolen cash, not unless he records all the serial numbers. And that's up to you to learn."

"She'll have me arrested! We'll all be caught, caught dead!"

"We all are eventually," Shelby murmured philosophically. "The grave's our one trap we cannot escape, much as we fear it."

"You're an optimistic bastard," Bishop observed.

He stood dripping a moment longer, then settled back down with a sigh of defeat, and listened to the others conjure up various half-baked schemes. He'd have to see Heloise again, he supposed; it'd be poison, but at least the cockeyed heist would collapse just as soon as he confronted her, of that he was sure.

Oddly, his certainty brought him no relief.

CHAPTER 16

The cobbled drive to the Algernon mansion scaled a low bluff overlooking Canta Lupe, breached the wrought-iron fence between two posterns, and looped in a circle as it threaded the entrance's porte cochere. When Bishop arrived at the porte cochere, he untied the dress boxes from his saddle skirt, flipped the reins around a brass hitching post, and mounted the steps to the Spanish-carved front door.

A middle-aged Papago housekeeper answered his tug of the bell cord. Bishop fully expected she would take the boxes and close the door, and then he'd ride back to town and that would be that. Instead she ushered him inside, her placid face having only the merest hint of expression that the likes of Bishop couldn't possibly be admitted through the front entry, and if so, then he shouldn't be.

She led him along a wide parquetry-floored hallway, into a room which was empty for the moment. It had large damask couches and lounging chairs arranged around a fireplace, over which hung an oil portrait of Ichabod Algernon. The late, unlamented banker looked as he had when alive, as if suffering from ten ingrown toenails all at once. Other paintings covered the walls, bouquets of dried flowers dotted the tables, and a curtained row of French doors opened out onto a rear terrace. The whole setup reeked of money and a lack of imagination.

The housekeeper, departing, left the inner door slightly open, as though to be able to hear if Bishop tried to filch the silver. A few minutes later, Heloise entered. Her hat and jacket were off, displaying her coiled hair and white silk blouse, but otherwise she was dressed as she had been when he'd first spotted her that noon.

"Two-thirty. You're punctual, I see, and I must say, much more presentable." Her voice was a shade louder and cooler than was necessary. She glanced at her boxes where Bishop had laid them on a table. "Yes, thank you. And would you kindly do me a favor?"

"If I can," Bishop replied, forcing a smile. "I didn't realize who you were before, Mrs. Algernon. I was terrible rude."

Their eyes met, and Bishop thought he detected a slight softening in them and her lips as she said, "Apology accepted." Then she moved on toward the French doors. "Are you seeking work?"

"Oh no, ma'am, me 'n' my partners are very busy."

"Good labor is so difficult to find these days." She unlatched one door and went outside. "May I ask what you do?"

"Ah . . . Investments. Mining, chiefly. Grub-staking."

"That explains your earlier appearance," she sniffed, closing the door behind him, and Bishop noticed that once again she was acting the capable, aloof matriarch. "I hope you've been successful?"

"Very. We're scouting for a solid bank, in fact."

"How coincidental. My husband heads the Canta Lupe Bank & Trust." She swept on ahead, across the terrace and down a flight of flagstone steps. "I'm sure he can be of great service to you."

"I'm sure," Bishop allowed deadpan, gratified yet surprised how she kept feeding him openings and curious why she kept raising her voice the further they drew from the house. "We're concerned about safety, though. Often our deposits are in gold and silver."

"Ease your mind. Our bank is protected by guards and the most modern security devices, and hasn't been robbed in, oh, twenty-five years."

"An enviable record."

"Yes, and it wouldn't have happened then, if it'd been attempted by strangers." She stopped before the small, stone statue of a garden dwarf. "Can you carry this around to my front plot?"

He nodded; the statue appeared to weigh all of ten pounds.

"It was robbed by four local riffraff," she continued, as though he hadn't agreed, or indeed, she hadn't even asked her question. "Disreputable thugs who took advantage of our charity, they were. Well, we've measures now to prevent any more undesirable elements."

Bishop eyed her, flinching slightly. Heloise was not looking at him, but was staring up at the house, whose lower floors were cut off from view by the angle of the long steps and the broad terrace.

The afternoon sun cameoed her face, highlighting her still youthful skin with its faint spattering of freckles across her snub nose. Pixieish, he'd once termed it, he thought, and it was true.

Abruptly she turned and regarded him, her voice dropping low and gentle yet faintly quivering. "Pick it up, Matt, please hurry."

Bishop stiffened. "What?"

"Forgive me, Matt, I know I've been an old witch. I had to be, had to use the boxes as an excuse, to get you here without raising suspicions. Please, take the statue, before she begins wondering."

He lifted it and found it weighed closer to twenty pounds.

"I'm sorry. It was the only thing down here, where we're out of her sight." Heloise started walking, Bishop falling in beside her. "She spies on me and reports everything she hears and sees."

Bishop frowned, perplexed. "The housekeeper?"

"Junius is so jealous of his possessions. And greedy, too," she said, as though this explained everything. "Oh, I'm pleased you're here, Matt, even for a little while. I thought you were dead."

"So did I, at least to folks here."

"Nobody'd know you—nobody who didn't know the lines around your eyes. Outlawing's done plenty to you, Matt. Were you and your friends ever caught? That marshal was always hot after you."

Bishop shook his head, but said nothing. The shallow footpath ran in a meandering course parallel to the rear of the house, and they were almost to the corner when Heloise said wistfully, "Remember in summer, when we'd lie out in the fields, and I'd trace all those lines with a piece of grass or straw? My, a lot's happened since then."

"An awful lot. P'raps too much, Mrs. Algernon."

Heloise lowered her eyes. "I deserve that. It was horrid, not telling you about Junius, even when the marriage was all set. I'm sure I . . . I'm to blame some for your hard life." She looked at him then, pleading, and her voice was small. "Matt, I didn't do it on purpose, to lead you on. I didn't know how to tell you."

"Hell, I doubt I'd have known how to take it if you had told me," he said gruffly. "You had your reasons, that was enough."

"I had good reasons. Daddy spoiled me rotten and could afford it, and I felt my husband should too. A good house, a good position, a good time, a good life. I resented you for being dirt poor—no, for me having to be dirt poor with you—and Junius could give me all my good things. We were both greedy as pigs."

"Well, you both got what you wanted, then."

"That's the irony. Junius didn't, because he can't ever get enough, can't ever grow big enough, to satisfy his wanting. I didn't, because my wants were the whims of a girl, not the needs of a woman."

"So you've made a new list," Bishop said curtly. "The women I've known all want what you've got, and they call them needs, too."

"Matt, a woman may want a fancy house, but she needs a home. She may want a wealthy man, but she needs a loving husband, one she can respect for who he is, not what he has. A woman may want to be a grand lady, but she needs to be a wife and maybe a mother, who's loved and respected in her own right and who . . . who respects herself."

She averted her head while reaching for a handkerchief.

"Learn from your mistakes, Heloise, don't weep over 'em."

"I wish I could cry," she murmured. "I wish I could let out some of what's inside me, if only tears, before I simply explode."

She faced him, and Bishop saw that her eyes were red-rimmed but dry. He studied her critically as they continued along the side of the mansion. He perceived a genuine anguish and frustration in her features, but he couldn't determine if they stemmed from a girl feeling self-pity, or a woman seeking maturity. So although she wasn't trying to trick him, she still could be fooling herself, which would inevitably result in more of the same pain . . . if he cared. He was in no position to care and in no mood to allow himself to care.

The path curved out in a wide horseshoe, snaking through a clump of boulders before winding toward the front of the mansion. There was a small clearing midway among the boulders, which would've made a cozy picnic rendezvous on warm evenings, but which on an early July afternoon, was a broiling caldron. Its one advantage was that it was concealed from the house, so Heloise called for a short break.

"Soon as we come around to the front, you'll have to plant the statue and leave," she told Bishop. "We'll probably not see each other again, and there're a couple of things I want to tell you."

Bishop laid the statue down and flexed his arms, waiting.

"First, it's taken me many years to do what I did today," she said, breaking an awkward silence. "You've always been independent, but I've always been provided for, and to even secretly defy Junius by sneaking you up here is like, well, like going behind my father's back. I'm trying to learn from my mistakes, Matt; I'm trying to solve them, to work my way out from them, but it's hard."

"And long overdue. But it comes easier with practice."

"So I'm finding. Y'see, the second thing just cropped up." She nudged the statue with her boot toe. "I know why you're here, Matt, you 'n' your friends. You're planning to rob the bank again."

Bishop laughed softly.

"Those questions you were asking me, they told me. Alright, you want to know about the bank's security? I'll answer you."

"You already have."

"Strictly for the housekeeper's benefit. Actually, the bank's about the way it always was. There're phones now, and their junction box is in the hall near Junius's office. So is the box for the electric alarm bell. One old guard, older'n the one before. The only surpriser is a khaki currency strongbox in the vault, conspicuously left unlocked and booby-trapped to explode. Junius's idea, so it's there."

"That figures. Hours?"

"Same ten to four. You'll make it."

"New locks, time locks, serial-number lists, like that?"

"Same old vault. Same combination too, I think. No lists or suchlike. Junius's too conceited to take precautions he didn't invent."

"Now listen, I don't want you mixed up in this."

"I hoped you'd say that," she said softly. "Maybe you think I'm a conniver, a betrayer. I'm not. I don't believe in the end justifying the means, but this once I do. It's my stab at breaking out, of fighting free. But y'see, I'm scared of doing it alone."

"Don't put yourself down, Heloise. You can do anything you want or need, but you won't till you stop expecting other people to provide your needs." Bishop picked up the statue again. "Start doing your doings later. Today and tomorrow, come what may, act normal."

He began to walk from the clearing, but she caught his arm. "I'm being honest with you, Matt. I truly do want to make amends."

They locked eyes, hers candid and hopeful, his reluctant and wary. There was no denying her eagerness, her yearning, or his own perverse attraction for her beguiling garden path. Nor was there denying her sensual fragrance, the hushed pulse of her breathing, the taut curve of her breasts as she swayed closer. Bishop focused on her carmine lips, moist and slightly parted, and he began bending . . .

He caught himself and straightened, irritated at himself for having weakened. "C'mon, your watchdog'll be snooping for us," he growled. "And don't make no amendings, no apologizing, Heloise. Look to the future, 'cause our past is ancient history, dead 'n' buried."

Riding back to town, Bishop tried to concentrate on the future, namely the proposed bank robbery. He'd spent longer with Heloise than he'd expected, so the timing would be extremely tight here on out. Yet to his amazement, he was returning with the necessary information, and assuming that the others were ready as planned, he suspected they'd actually try to pull off this harebrained heist.

He found he was feeling jumpy about it. He couldn't exactly pinpoint it, for it wasn't strong like anxiety or fear; it was as though he was twitched, and no longer merely involved because he didn't have anything better to do. He wondered if it had to do with his determination that Heloise didn't come to grief because of it. But the more he mulled it over, the more he grew convinced that it was from the relished anticipation of stripping Junius to his skin.

He also found that if he didn't concentrate, his mind would wander from the future back to the past, where Heloise and his affections had died and been buried. For twenty-five years he'd held down the lid on that coffin, eventually ceasing to be haunted and virtually forgetting it was there. But he'd tampered with its grave by returning here. He'd kept it fairly well covered with a polite reserve, until the very last when something got loose and nearly got him. He'd managed to contain it again, he thought, but he couldn't deny its existence . . . not to his own mind, at least. . . .

Canta Lupe was torpid in the blistering heat of mid-afternoon, when Bishop tethered his horse at the Northern Lights and walked down Main Street. What activity stirred was mostly centered around watching the bus arrive from El Paso. Rumbling and thrashing, steam geysering from its radiator, the eight-window White motorbus parked for its stopover alongside the El Victorio restaurant.

Bishop elbowed his way through the listless group of onlookers and passengers, almost bowling into the shirt-sleeved ticket seller as the man set up his A-board smack in the middle of the boardwalk:

GREAT SOUTHWESTERN
AUTOCOACH LINES
Phoenix-El Paso

He met his three partners in the freight alley behind Shirmer's Pharmacy. Crandon and LeRoy were waiting in the dilapidated wagon rented from the livery. Shelby was returning from a last-minute errand at Shirmer's and accompanied Bishop to the wagon, which was a low, box-type with wobbly wheels, harnessed to a spavined dun mare.

Crandon, the master planner, was fretting exactly as he had on the previous job, two and a half decades ago. "Damn, Matt, you're late!"

"Hell, I am," Bishop retorted, climbing up with Shelby. "The bank's got the same hours, so we're okay." Then swiftly he relayed Heloise's information, omitting how he'd learned it. Considering what the others thought of Heloise, his coup sounded better than it was.

Even Crandon was heartened. "You brung us the right news, Matt. Reckon you've earned a snort of this," he declared, offering Bishop his pint of Old Crow. "Now, assumin' the wheels stay on and the nag don't drop, I can't see any reason why our plan won't work."

"Well, Shirmer's was out of adhesive bandage," Shelby said

glumly, taking the flask. "I had to buy hot-mustard chest plasters."

"Those'll work fine, Harold. Maybe better'n tape." Crandon surveyed the bed of the wagon. "Ropes, satchels, hatchet, burlap bags, and twine . . . Guffy? Aurora's expecting us, you're sure?"

"I'm sure," LeRoy answered, as Shelby handed him the whiskey. "She don't know why, of course, but she'll be a-waitin'."

Crandon eyed LeRoy apprehensively. "Go easy on that."

"A wee sip," LeRoy said, and upended the pint against his lips. The Old Crow gurgled, rapidly diminishing while Crandon yelped, "Stop him!" and Bishop finally snatched the bottle away.

Appalled, Crandon retrieved the dregs of his whiskey, then scowled at LeRoy. "You mis'rable boozer! You're gonna replace this pint outa your share or your hide, whichever I grab hold of first!"

LeRoy belched and daubed his mouth with his sleeve, a fresh, devilish spark flickering in his eyes. "Then, what're we sitting around here for? C'mon, let's go be gettin' all our shares!"

CHAPTER 17

First, Shelby left to check on the deputy again.

Returning shortly, he reported that Deputy Max was still occupied at the south edge with a two-buggy accident and subsequent fistfight. It was a lucky break, one they'd been avidly hoping for, since they hadn't been able to engineer a diversion on purpose.

After a few more minutes, Crandon judged the timing was about right for an inconspicuous stroll to the bank, thereby avoiding the possible suspicions which rushing or dawdling can attract. LeRoy took over the wagon reins while the others climbed down with their satchels. Suitcases, cabinet bags, even gladstones would've served equally well; it just so happened the secondhand store had three brown leather satchels, which were now stuffed full and quite heavy.

The trio sauntered along Main Street, arriving at the bank entrance within seconds of closing. They paused until the elderly guard inside approached to lock the front door, and then barged in, barking his shin painfully against the door. It took a while to help him up, dust his uniform, and finish their profuse apologies.

Canta Lupe Bank & Trust's interior was of plaster, varnished wainscoting, the flag and a picture of Woodrow Wilson, and not much else. It was bisected by a row of wickets, and a pair of partitions in the back separated the vault area and Algernon's office.

The lobby was deserted, though a few late customers wouldn't have made much difference, because the handful of staff was still exiting by a rear door. Stalling until they'd all left was a simple matter of assuring the guard the appointment with Algernon could wait till his shin was better, the door was locked, and the shades drawn.

When it had thinned down to the guard, Algernon in his office, and Algernon's private secretary, who sat at a desk by the hallway to Algernon's office, Crandon said cheerily, "Let's get to business."

Nodding to the guard, they started across to the secretary. Halfway, Shelby snapped his fingers as though he'd thought of something, and headed back toward the guard, reaching him at the same time that Crandon and Bishop stopped in front of the secretary.

The secretary was a thin, weedy chap with slicked hair and a green eyeshade. He glanced up, readying to simper and say no.

"Algernon around?" Crandon asked politely.

"In his office." The secretary smiled ingratiatingly. "Oh, but I'm afraid he's frightfully busy at the moment. Maybe tomorrow."

"Then you'll do," Bishop said and drew his revolver.

The secretary blinked. "Are you threatening me?"

"Promising," Bishop snarled. "Get up and around here."

While the secretary was easing out from his desk, licking dry lips and eyeing the leveled revolver, Shelby was talking to the guard. "Y'know," he said conversationally, "I never knew the bank had a nest of fruit bats right inside here."

"Bats?" the guard said. "Where?"

Shelby pointed casually toward the far corner. "Up there."

The guard turned his head. In one swift second, Shelby lifted his plow-handled Colt from its holster and backed off. "Don't make a move, I don't want to harm you," he said quietly.

The guard swiveled around anyway, staring first at Shelby and then across at the secretary's desk, where Crandon was saying the same thing Shelby had. "We don't want to harm you."

But the secretary was a disbeliever. He moved close enough

to Bishop to stomp hard on his instep and then sprang lunging to wrestle away Bishop's revolver. It was a silly and short-lived defiance. While Shelby and the guard stood bewilderedly watching, Bishop ripped his revolver free and Crandon punched the secretary alongside the right temple. The secretary spun and folded across his desk, stunned but not out, his arms flailing papers and overturning the inkwell, its spilled ink soaking into his ready-made suit.

Holstering his revolver, Bishop helped Crandon march the dazed secretary through the teller section. The guard, needing no prompting, followed with Shelby. The square vault door was closed but unlocked, and when Shelby had swung it ajar, he returned for his satchel while Bishop and Crandon ushered their two prisoners inside.

The interior of the vault was like a cramped, musty hollow. Bishop and Crandon ignored its contents for the moment, and when Shelby returned, set to work roping the secretary and guard to a metal pole support, wrists and ankles, back to back. Shelby opened one of the mustard plasters and slapped it across the secretary's mouth.

"I got a powerful tender skin," the guard said, without much hope. "Like a baby's, it is, an' my moustache is shedding hair."

"We'll make it easy for you," Shelby said, and the guard nodded his appreciation. "But we'll be around awhile, so no noise."

"The young are rash," the guard said, as the trio left the vault. "Me, I've been around long enough to be smart about things."

Shelby poked his head out the rear door and gestured at LeRoy, who was waiting down the freight alley a short distance. Meanwhile, Bishop removed the hatchet from his satchel and chopped the phone and alarm-bell lines apart in their junction boxes.

"Maybe we should've cut the lines earlier, before we did anything with the guard and secretary," Crandon said. "If anything had happened, Algernon could've rung to the rescue."

"Six o' one, an' half dozen of another," Bishop replied, coming to Algernon's office door. "You get a feisty idiot like that secretary, and you've gotta take him out of action pronto."

The men went in without knocking.

Hunched behind his massive mahogany desk, Junius Algernon was too absorbed in his torpedo cigar and thick entry ledger to pay any attention. "Whatever it is, the answer's no."

Bishop reached down over the open ledger, yanked Algernon's cigar out and crumbled tobacco, ash, and cinder into the banker's lap.

"What's the meaning of—" Algernon started shouting, straightening in a leap and slapping his suit and vest, his gold watch chain bouncing like a looped fringe across his paunch. Then he caught sight of the drawn revolvers and then of their owners.

"You!" His eyes bulged and his hands froze on his vest.

"Surprise!" Bishop grinned tightly and, holstering his revolver again as he circled the desk, he started giving Algernon a shakedown. "And I just bet you've got a surprise for us too," he added, and grunting confirmation, removed a .32 H&R hammerless pistol from Algernon's hip pocket. Slipping it into one of his own pockets, Bishop stood there beside Algernon and basked in the hatred glaring back.

"You shouldn't have come back, Matt," Algernon snarled and turned his fuming glance to Crandon. "You either, Emmett. There's nothing here for you 'cept a heavy dose of belated justice."

"Why, damned if we didn't hear boom times were happenin' here," Crandon replied mockingly. "Rich pots to be had, even fatter'n yours."

Algernon stuck his thumbs pompously behind his watch chain and bristled with indignation, the florid blush of his cheeks deepening when Bishop added, "Must be Junius's steady diet of liens and foreclosures that's making him so heavy and able to throw his weight around."

"Very well, you've had your fun. Ha, ha. Now get out!"

"We don't joke where money's concerned, Junius."

Algernon's eyes narrowed and glinted like shards of dark glass, and his hands squeezed around the thick chain links as though exercising for a certain pair of human necks. "You won't get away with it."

"Damn," Bishop growled disgustedly, turning around to walk away. "Can't you think of anything more original than that, Junius?"

Suddenly, with an adroit flick of his wrist, Algernon whipped his pocket watch out by its chain, and spun it twirling in a fast arc. The thick gold case clubbed Bishop just behind one ear, and Bishop staggered forward a few rubbery steps. His spurs caught on the Mexican-woven throw rug, which almost pitched him, but, reeling to keep upright, he kicked the rug free and pivoted to lash into Algernon.

Algernon whirled his watch to hammer Bishop another blow. Bishop, feinting, shifted Algernon's pitching aim off just enough to duck in from the other side. Starting somewhere down around his boots, Bishop shot his fist in a rocketing uppercut to the jaw.

Jolted off his feet, Algernon corkscrewed as he came down again, smashing his watch against the surface of the desk. The wood indented, turnip-shaped, and watch springs and gears showered out of the rupturing caseworks. And Algernon just kept on dropping, crumpling on his face between his desk keyhole and swivel chair.

Bishop and Crandon each grabbed a leg and dragged the unconscious banker outside and over to the vault. Using rope from Shelby's satchel, they added insult to injury by hog-tying Algernon, then dumping him on his side on the lid of the booby-trapped strongbox.

LeRoy was in the vault when they did this and watched with malicious laughter. The secretary gave one horrified look at his trussed employer and went berserk, wrenching on his bindings and nearly swallowing his mustard plaster, until both LeRoy and the guard threatened to smack him a good one if he didn't behave.

"How's it going, Guffy?" Bishop asked, rubbing his head.

"See for yourself. I think this'll be our last load."

Glancing around, Bishop and Crandon eyed the empty shelving and rifled drawers. LeRoy, with a small gunnysack drooped open in one hand, was scooping the final stacks of currency from a top shelf, ignoring the rolls of coins and the carton of Mexican peso notes. The floor was littered with deeds, letters, certificates, and other personal effects that'd been scattered while looting the safety boxes.

"Harold's watching outside," LeRoy said, slinging the now full sack over a shoulder. "He's plumb the fastest at sewing the topseams on these sacks. Y'know, he mightn't make a bad li'le tailor."

Bishop told the guard, "We'll bolt the door, but won't spin the tumbler, so anyone tomorrow morning'll be able to let you out."

"Don't worry, we won't suffocate," the guard assured as they left. "We've even caught mice squeezing in here. We'll be dandy."

The vault door was closed and secured, and after their tools and satchels were all accounted for, the men fled to the wagon in the alley. Crandon took the reins, and as the horse sluggishly plodded forward, LeRoy groused, "What's a good holdup anyhow without a good getaway?"

"A sneaky but successful one," Shelby retorted. "Or'd you prefer a rousin' shoot-up like last time, with us leadin' the posse on a long merry chase to Aurora's? Or's she gonna ride with us?"

Shortly, Crandon cut the wagon over to Main, and they continued creeping up toward the Northern Lights. Teams and saddle horses and a few gas buggies ebbed and flowed along the street, their riders and the boardwalk pedestrians never suspecting that the four country bumpkins in the derelict wagon were hauling thousands in bank loot.

Braking in front of the Northern Lights, Crandon suggested: "Let's clean up the loose ends and then surprise Aurora."

The eight gunnysacks were carried in underarm and hidden behind the foyer counter, the desk clerk shrewdly turning a blind eye. LeRoy stayed to guard, while Crandon went searching for someone to return the livery's horse and wagon, and Shelby began checking over their horses, which were among the other mounts lining the front hitching rail.

Bishop hauled the satchels and leftover supplies around to the rear, where he buried them deep in the kitchen's overflowing garbage cans. He wasn't surprised to see the gaping barroom wall was not fixed. He was surprised to see a Hudson tourer parked near the flattened fence. Going back to the front, he joined Crandon and Shelby and went inside.

"Ended up payin' a guy to drive 'em down to the stable," Crandon said, as they lugged two sacks apiece up the stairs. "But abandonin' the wagon here would've been too bald, could've caused Aurora too much trouble. At worst now, even if the satchels are ever found, she can claim we were just hurrawin' customers passing through."

Aurora was knitting when she called for them to come in her room. She was an aggressive knitter, her needles clacking fiercely as they dumped the sacks on the floor. "Excuse me, boys, if I don't get up. One of m'girls is pregnant, and I'm late with some booties."

Bishop hunkered by her chair. "Aurora, where is she?"

"Went home to her mother's to have the baby."

"You know who I'm meanin', Aurora. And don't try telling me it was Junius or his chauffeur who's driven here a-visitin'."

"Ask me no questions, I'll tell you no lies."

"It's alright," Heloise said resignedly as she stepped in from the bedroom, and Bishop's partners let out a concerted groan.

"You're supposed to be home behavin' reg'ar," Bishop said, exasperated yet strangely pleased to see her again. "Having afternoon tea with the local madam ain't a usual habit of yours, is it?"

"You don't understand. I didn't understand, Matt, till I'd thought things through. I had to find you, to try'n stop you, but I didn't know where. Then I remembered Aurora, and how Guffy used to . . ." She drew a shaky breath, her eyes downcast. "You're right, this isn't normal at all. I can't think what's come over me."

Neither could three of the men. They stared, dumbfounded that the Heloise who'd chewed them apart at noon could be the same Heloise who now was so humble and imploring. But Bishop felt less bewildered than suspicious, leery of being burned again by any wheedling meek sighs and blandishing calf's eyes.

"Well, whatever you're understanding, you can forget," he said curtly, ripping open a sack. "You're too late to stop us."

"Oh, that's awful! The bank'll be ruined!"

Crandon chuckled. "We hit Junius where it hurt, okay."

"You didn't kill him, did you?" Aurora asked sharply, her needles pausing. When Bishop shook his head, she focused on him, watching while he dumped out and began counting the banded sheaves of currency. "Just what d'you think you're doing with all that green?"

"Don't sound so hard, Aurora. Some of it's for you."

"Over my dead body." The needles resumed with a clatter.

"But now you can pay off Junius," LeRoy argued. "He'll never figure it's his own cash. We made sure nobody'll ever suspect you."

"I couldn't care less about that! Guffy LeRoy, I could thump you silly with your own leg, and that holds for the rest of you, too!"

"What're you mad about?" Shelby asked. "We didn't rob you."

"Yes, you did," Heloise answered instead. "It's not like it was before, when only the few big farmers and ranchers dealt with the bank. Now most every family, every small shop, is a depositor. By robbing the bank, you're robbing everyone, including Aurora."

"Hell, if that's all, we'll kick in extra," LeRoy said.

"Besides, a bank's deposits are mostly tied up in loans 'n' land," Crandon added, shrugging. "Those're safe, and what we stole will be repaid. It might take Junius a time to liquidate enough assets, but—"

"That's the point," Heloise insisted. "He won't get the time. I've been a banker's wife for twenty-five years; I've seen what's happened to other small-town banks needing time. A run starts. The smaller depositors fear for their savings, and when they can't be fully paid on demand, rumors spread that the bank's going broke. The run becomes a panic, and then the bank really does have to close down."

"How'n hell do you expect us to stop it?" Bishop demanded, glancing up from his counting. "A people panic is like a cattle stampede—you just got to move aside and let 'er rip its course."

LeRoy nodded. "Yeah, let Junius borrow the money."

Heloise shook her head. "Not this much, this quickly."

"And boys, if the bank folds, much of Canta Lupe'll fold with it. No customers, no Northern Lights." Aurora glowered at the men. "I may not love my business, but I'd hate to be forced out of it."

"Say, where'll we go?" Shelby nervously asked, eager to change subjects. "I was kinda thinking of Mexico for a change."

"Are you kidding? Don't you read the papers? There's another revolution going on, and President Wilson's making noises about us intervening. Harold, this ain't the time to play the rich gringo!"

"Well, I'm damned sick of always going north!"

"Twenty-eight thousand, four hundred and four," Bishop announced proudly, stuffing money back into the sacks. "We can divvy it now or later, makes no difference to me."

LeRoy slumped glumly. "Now, and give my share to Aurora. I couldn't have no fun spendin' it, knowin' it was shutting the place."

"I'll return it to the bank," Aurora warned.

Bishop laughed. "There's a switch, handing Junius some of his own money back to help him pay withdrawals and not go bust."

"Then add my cut to the collection plate." Crandon said. "I don't need it. All the money I need, I can draw out of Torment."

Bishop glanced at Shelby, who looked too torn to make up his mind. He laughed again, scoffingly. "We'll toss it all in, Aurora. I'd just waste my share, like I blew it the first time. And Harold here don't want to be bulldogged by Deputy Max, the way ol' Tighe did before. Hell, twisting Junius by the short hairs was payment enough."

"I guess that settles where we'll go," Crandon said to Shelby, before Shelby could protest. "Way I figure, our current combined pot is roughly fifteen dollars, so let's go to Tucson."

From down Main Street came a sudden explosion—a thunderous, throaty eruption that jarred the Northern Lights on its foundation. A ceramic vase toppled off its stand and smashed on the floor, and Aurora nearly tipped over backward in her chair, her knitting flying from her grasp. Heloise and the men raced to the windows.

"Earthquake?" LeRoy suggested, lifting a sash.

"More like dynamite," Crandon replied as he struggled to raise the other window. "Three or four sticks at once of it."

"The bank!" Shelby yelled, and they all craned heads out.

Main Street was a turmoil of rushing feet and shouting alarm. The bank building was percolating smoke from under its eaves and out shattered windows. Its front door was lying in the street, surrounded by a blast pattern of glass shards and shredded papers.

By some fluke, nobody appeared seriously injured. The guard had lost his cap and was bending, coughing to clear his lungs. The disheveled secretary was lurching about, both hands clawing at the stubborn mustard plaster. Junius was weaving just outside the entrance, arms flapping as if trying to take off.

Mostly he was wearing red cotton longjohns, though tatters of shirt and suit were clinging around his neck, wrists, and ankles. The trapdoor of his johns was open, displaying the only exposed skin that wasn't blackened with soot.

"Can't be!" LeRoy blurted. "How'd they get loose?"

"Looks like Junius blew them out with his booby trap," Bishop said. "Not that I reckon on going down there and asking for details."

Heloise nodded. "No, you get to riding!"

"We can't," Shelby moaned. "There go our horses."

They stared where he was pointing, up the opposite direction where Main Street became the road leaving town. Galloping away in a wide flurry of dust were all the horses from the hitching rail out front. They were still tied to the rail, but the rail was no longer out front; apparently the explosion had shaken the support posts so violently that the frightened horses, rearing and fishing, had been able to suck the whole caboodle right out of the ground. Now they were off and running literally neck-and-neck, an eleven-horse team on a single, long harness.

"Not a horse to steal anywhere nearby," Crandon said grimly, surveying the street again. "We'll have to head for the livery."

"Let's do it while we can, then," Shelby said. "That crowd down there looks about ready to spread out searching for us."

"Yeah, we hafta hightail fast." LeRoy turned from the window and crossed to Aurora. "I'll be back," he said, bending low and kissing her long and slowly, putting emphasis in it. "Bank on it."

Bishop, ducking inside, bumped against Heloise. She made no move to pull away but stood close, her hips up against his thigh so he could feel the pulse of her blood. "Matt, steal my car."

"Nice idea, 'cept none of us've ever driven."

She placed her hand on his mouth. Tensely she explained how to start and run the Hudson, something akin to tears filming her eyes. "It's not fair. You're having to risk your life to get nothing."

Her hand lowered and he grinned. "It's my life."

Her breath was a hiss as she lifted on her toes to whisper in his ear, "Take good care of it, Matt. It's mine now, too."

CHAPTER 18

The men eased downstairs, wary of being trapped in the foyer by cross fire from the wings. But scarcely any attention was paid to them, those concerned or sober enough to be interested having already gone, adding to the din and confusion around the bank.

The men hastened through the barroom and out the large hole in the rear wall, hearing the yells and shouts and aware that soon the hunt would begin. Each passing second lessened their chances of escape, and odds were that by now every horse was being watched.

That left only the Hudson.

Bishop eyed it distrustfully. "Stand back, I don't know what it'll do, and there's no need for more'n me to get trampled."

"Hell, we won't even get throwed," LeRoy said, as they all accompanied Bishop to the car. "You'll tame 'er first time outa the chute, Matt. You're the best roper an' breaker around, remember?"

"I remember a lot of things you've claimed," Bishop growled, climbing in behind the wheel. LeRoy sat with Shelby in the back, while Crandon took the passenger seat and helped Bishop locate things.

"Heloise told it something like this," Bishop said, and acted out her instructions as he repeated them. "You step on both its feet here, put this handle here, pull out these two buttons, and yank down on these levers. Then pull this, and it should start up."

Nobody could hear the last of what Bishop was saying, because the Hudson was spitting and roaring with life by then. "Let'er rip!" Bishop shouted, popping the clutch and stomping on the gas pedal.

The Hudson lurched forward, almost flinging LeRoy over the side. Shelby pulled him in, yelling at the same time to Bishop, "You're going the wrong way! We want to go *out* of town!"

But the Hudson continued buck-jumping down Main, sending pedestrians diving frantically out of its erratic path. It swapped ends twice, skirting a buckboard and barely missing the side of the parked motorbus. The angry cries of the bus driver were lost as Bishop corrected the steering too much, and the Hudson bounded up onto the boardwalk and through the double-doored entrance of the El Victorio. He made three circles of the center settee in the lobby, surged along a corridor on two wheels, and burst out into the freight alley. Up the alley and over to Main on a cross street he slued, clipping loading platforms, dodging refuse barrels, squashing cartons, and splintering crates.

Turning back onto Main in a four-wheel drift, Bishop glimpsed men closing in full chase. Deputy Max came lunging out of the crowd in front of the bank, revolver in fist. The Hudson steamed past him, and his wrathful bellow of recognition curdled in the afternoon heat. His angry snap shot ricocheted off the radiator ornament; and further enraged by his poor marksmanship, the deputy commandeered the first car that came along, a farmer's open-bodied Ford T, the farmer and his family forced to get out while the deputy and a few select marksmen scrambled in.

"Put the spurs to 'er, Matt!" Shelby advised, after a second shot shattered the windshield. "Deputy Max is on the rampage!"

"Don't worry," Bishop called back. "I got 'er trained to my touch now, and she's a Thoroughbred in the stretch."

Bishop goosed the throttle, and the Hudson tore up Main Street, quivering and howling. The deputy punched the Ford into hot pursuit, with one man hanging out one door and another clinging to the rear deck panel. They crawled in, and the chase was on.

Bishop was still accelerating as he passed Canta Lupe's town limits. The irony of it all had not escaped him—they'd arrived poor and left poorer, having grubstaked the bank after robbing it bare, their departure the same as the last time they'd quit town, in frantic haste, pursued by a gun-bristling posse.

Town faded behind the quickening Hudson. The deputy's borrowed Ford was keeping pace, they saw, with galloping horsemen strung out almost all the way back to Main Street. One by one the horsemen dropped away, mounts flagging, exhausted by the excessive speed.

The gradual loss of support only seemed to strengthen Deputy Max's determination. His riders began taking turns popping up, standing and swaying while they aimed and fired over his head, then sitting down for the next man. Accuracy was impossible, but the road surface was even enough to allow a good peppering of the general target.

Holes were drilled in the Hudson's body and canvas, lead whining past uncomfortably close, one slug burning along Bishop's left arm and raising a welt. Before the rifles could do any more damage, he swung the wheel sharply and launched the Hudson bounding across the flat. Crandon clung to the dashboard to steady himself, but LeRoy and Shelby took more of a tossing, shaking and sprawling and flopping over each other, the Hudson gaining momentum with every jump.

The nimble Ford sailed off the road and descended like a coiling spring, squatting low and then leaping clear of the ground. The riders were all churned around ass over elbow, gouging thumbs and muzzles into eyes, ears, and noses. The deputy embraced the steering post and waited while the Ford hopped three more times, knocking his chin against the hub, before the Ford stopped vibrating.

As Bishop had hoped, the surrounding basin was too cracked and corrugated to allow decent shooting, the men in the Ford staying down, if not always seated, and saving their ammunition. Except for scattered patches of brush, the terrain was fairly open, so both cars were able to storm along without much trouble, and for a while it seemed it'd be a matter of who ran out of gas first.

Shortly, however, the ground grew more rugged as the basin rose toward the Shadrack Hills. The Hudson veered across the lip and up into the barrancas and banks that Bishop knew from childhood. A moment later, the Ford braced the same stretch of slopes a-flying, and began drawing nearer as the Hudson started to buck-jump and sputter. Bishop pedaled and shifted with precision born of desperation, and the Hudson responded with resurgent power, bursting over the first rise in full roar.

Deputy Max was close behind but over a bit, having spotted what he considered to be a faster route up. Puffing and wheezing, the Ford crested the hill and catapulted into a wild boar's nest. The sow tried to ram the invader while piglets scurried for cover, but was still whirling around when the Ford's two off-wheels rolled up and over her brisket, leaving her unhurt but mighty upset. The angled impact with her, however, caught one of the riders napping; he was chucked out into a prickly-pear patch before anyone could grab him. The Ford rattled on without a pause, and the man, shouting, sprinted after it. The sow lumbered after him, and the man abruptly changed his mind and scrambled in another direction.

The deputy swung across to cut into the trail of the fleeing Hudson. The chase continued at breakneck gait through scalloped gullies and across stone tables and over crumbly, scrub-infested hills. The Hudson had more power, but the Ford had more agility, and no sooner than one would gain an advantage than the landscape would alter, and the other would have the upper hand.

They reached the far side of the Shadrack Hills with no change in their respective positions. They plunged down the steep, sandy bank of a wash, which sloughed and slid and gave way under churning wheels, filling the air with boiling dust.

Deputy Max and his men got the worse of it, only because they were so close behind the Hudson. But the resolute lawman merely pawed the grit off his face and kept his accelerator pegged to the floorboards, ignoring the wheezing and spitting and parch-lipped cursing around him.

Across a low washboard plain they dashed, the shimmery lane of the Tucson-Las Cruces roadway like a goal line in the near distance. The pink monstrosity of Dimwiddy's Desert Museum hovered on the left, but Bishop had no intention of stopping there, gas pump or no. He angled instead on a tangent that would pass its rear yard, thinking to intercept the roadway diagonally, heading in the direction of Tucson.

"This time," he shouted to the others, "we'll beat the Ford on the straight stretches. We've got it in the bag!"

Deputy Max was not about to let that happen if he could help it. With daring and resourcefulness, he nursed more speed out of the Ford, crossing a rocky section that could have sliced his tires, while Bishop played it safe by curving around it.

Of a sudden, just as the Hudson was clipping by the little fence around Dimwiddy's backyard, Bishop saw Deputy Max bearing in from the side. The deputy's intentions were obvious: he was going to ram the Hudson if need be, while the Hudson was trapped between the fence and the Ford, with no room to turn.

"Hold on!" Bishop yelled, and downshifted for more power, swerving away to avoid the brunt of a collision. There was a crunch of front fender, and the shattering of a headlamp, the Ford striking the Hudson a glancing blow. Bishop hit the fence, splintering the crossbeams and tearing into the museum's display area. The deputy circled around and bowled through after him, convinced now that he had the Hudson cornered.

Bishop speared down an aisle of display cages, while the deputy darted like a whippet to overtake and block him. The museum's back lot and corral were swarming with hysterical sightseers, men howling, women wailing and dragging crying children every which way. The Hudson ripped across another aisle, toppling cases and breaking tables, trundling along as if it were a rogue elephant being attacked by a coyote. The riders with the deputy tried to zero in on the Hudson whenever they could catch it alone. Bishop zigzagged evasively, ignoring the spurting rifles; jouncing and swerving the way they were, the shooters still couldn't aim for sour apples.

The two autos slued faster with each turn, circling and swapping ends. Snakes, spiders, toads, and scorpions scuttled about thicker than fleas on a Georgian hound. Jackrabbits, sage hens, tortoises and a stray warthog galloped and flapped to get out of the way. Chaos reigned, people running out of the building only to run back inside, not knowing what to do or where to hide to avoid the released animals, rampaging cars, and potshot bullets.

Bishop wasn't sure how to get out of it, either. The inside of the Hudson sang with lead, glass shattering into tiny slivers and the seats puncturing like pincushions. He crouched very low, only his hands above window height so he could steer.

"What're you doing down there?" Crandon yelled. "We'll crash!"

"No, we won't. I'm looking through the bullet holes!" Glancing up, Bishop thought of another bright idea. "Em, unbuckle the top! Harold, Guffy, help him lift it off the windshield frame!"

The three wrestled with the rig, popping it free just as Bishop tore into a long aisle, the Ford breathing down its trunk. Two thirds of the way along, when it was rolling at a good clip, the wind finally caught the top and opened it like an umbrella. The top sheared loose at the back, fluttered free in the air currents for a moment, then came slowly down to envelop the Ford. Deputy Max and his men tried valiantly to thrash their way clear of the cloaking shroud, but not in time, and they ran head-on into a coop full of gila monsters.

The Hudson's canvas top was jolted and rolled off, and the Ford filled up with gila monsters as it highballed through the length of the coop and out the other end. Behind was a signboard held upright by a wire clothesline, which snagged on the

Ford's windshield, drawing tight like a pulled bowstring and wrenching a corner support bracket off the building. The other end of the wire was anchored to a solid post, so the bracket sprang up to the windshield and smashed the glass, then hooked on the windshield stanchion and yanked the Ford around. Deputy Max lurched half off his seat, and the bracket snapped free of the stanchion and hoisted the deputy out by his suspenders. He tumbled through the air as the Ford chugged up a ramp to the building, dropping off gila monsters along the way.

With a grinding screech, the driverless Ford squeezed through a doorway and into the building, where it smacked dead-center into a glass cabinet of Indian pottery shards. The astounded riders were hurled out in a salvo, the cabinet disintegrated into fragments of glass, wood, and clay, and the Ford rolled over on its back, smoke and steam belching from both ends, and expired.

Crowds formed, epitaphs raged, and a fistfight or two broke out. And Bishop zoomed lickety-split out of the corral exit, crossing over onto the roadway as if the Hudson were on fire.

"I wouldn't have believed it," Crandon sighed, "if I hadn't seen it."

Bishop kept the Hudson barreling west, toward Tucson. He knew, as they all knew, that such routes as this were actually chains of shorter roads linking towns and settlements and old relay stations every ten or fifteen miles apart. He tried to remember the name of the next spot along the road, but finally gave up and asked. Shelby seemed to recollect it was a tiny village called Valle, but nothing else, and Bishop didn't press it.

Through the burning heat of the late afternoon they drove, enveloped in a wheel-churning nimbus of glistening dust and sand-like gypsum. They entered a patch of scarps and gullies, which soon broadened into a valley shaded by spindly cottonwoods. Ahead, clustered about a stone-wall well, could be seen old, deteriorating adobe buildings, their mud-colored bricks blending with the ocher terrain.

Bishop pulled over and stopped, idling, relieved that so far nobody appeared to be pursuing them. Not that he had illusions that they were safe. "Telephones, telegraphs, they're faster'n we are," he told the others. "I don't see any lines running into Valle, but that doesn't mean they haven't been alerted about us."

"Yeah, and if they haven't been," Crandon added, "they soon will be, and'll report having spotted this chariot passing through."

"So what do we do?" Shelby asked.

LeRoy said, "Hell, easy. We'll go 'round, cross country."

"No, we're about out of gas anyway, Guffy." Bishop stroked his chin. "We'll ditch it and go get us something else to ride."

"Sure," LeRoy retorted. "And since we ain't got the money, we'll just steal us something else, which won't cause no alarm a'tall."

"Not quite," Bishop said, grinning. "Not quite . . ."

He refused to elaborate, turning around and driving back to the rim of the valley. He cut off and slowly bumped over rocks and crevices, keeping parallel to the valley for a short distance until he braked next to a narrow ravine. "Last stop, everybody out!"

"Why wreck it?" Shelby asked, climbing down. "It won't take 'em all that longer to find it down at the bottom, y'know."

Crandon shook his head. "No, Harold, Matt's right. If it takes 'em ten extra minutes, it's worth one to roll it over."

"Hell, let's get it done and over," LeRoy said and put his shoulder to the doorjamb. "I'm hot 'n' thirsty, and we still gotta walk."

The others joined him, and heaving together, ran the Hudson off the edge. It rolled down the steep incline with surprising sedateness, scraping against boulders and tipping dangerously, but managing to stay on all four wheels until it crunched into the rock and sand-choked bottom, plowing forward a few more feet and then resting.

LeRoy regarded it disgustedly. "Kinda disappointin', that."

Twenty minutes later, they were trudging wearily into Valle. Most of the village was of small, single-story adobe dwellings, with protruding weathered beams and earth-coated thatch roofs. Around them were brush-covered ramadas and pens fenced by stacked cholla branches. Children, dogs, and goats romped in the dusty plaza about the well, while Mexican, white, and ladino adults lazily conversed in as much Indian and Spanish as English.

Bishop led the way to the largest building, which was long and roofed with a front gallery, and was obviously the village's general store, post office, cantina, and community center. They ordered beers, and after the bartender was finished with that, Bishop said to him, "We need four tickets on the next bus west."

"To where?" the bartender asked, removing his apron.

Before Bishop could answer, LeRoy bellowed, "A *motorbus?*"

"Sure, Guffy. Who'd ever think we'd take one, eh?"

"I, for one! But, well . . . If it's the only way, I guess."

"It's that, or we walk," Bishop assured him, and turned to the bartender, who'd put on an eyeshade and become the ticket agent. "Tucson," he told him, "or however far ten bucks will take us."

"Tucson." The agent began writing out the tickets. "A Grea' Sou'western Autocoach will be here in a few hours, the only one today."

They waited inside, which was boring, but was pleasantly cool and dim, and close to food and booze. They went outside when it became cooler with approaching dusk, however, and walked around the side of the building, where they could sit and watch without being watched. There'd been no posses or lawmen stopping or rushing through, not even one lousy badge-toter so far, and the tranquillity was getting on their nerves. The sun continued its slow decline, sending out scarlet streamers and gilding the silhouette of distant peaks. But the pending glories of evening held little interest; they kept wondering if a nasty surprise wasn't being hidden elsewhere.

"That was damn smart, Matt, thinking of a motorbus," Crandon said, producing a pint flask from his pocket and opening it.

"No, I recalled the one I almost clobbered in Canta Lupe, is all, and that it was heading in the direction we want to go."

LeRoy spotted the bottle. "Ah! Pass it here, pal."

"Not so fast. If you want a drink, it's only to the neck."

The whiskey in the neck was about a thimble's worth. Grimacing, LeRoy snatched the bottle from Crandon and swallowed until the level fell to the label.

"You soaker! Don't drink it all!"

"Almost made me drop it, you did." Reproachfully swigging again, he handed the bottle back. "Well, I'll take a horse any day."

"Horses don't have the speed or stamina of a good motorcar." Crandon himself nipped at the whiskey. "We proved that, didn't we?"

"We could've rode in the hills 'n' never've been found."

"Maybe, but progress is making it more difficult all the time. Big changes in twenty-five years, okay. Here, the last is yours."

"I wouldn't have been found." LeRoy scrutinized the empty bottle for clinging drops. Then he scowled, and then he flung the bottle at Crandon. "Damn your eyes, that was *my* bottle!"

"Serves you fair for guzzling mine before." Chuckling, Crandon backed away. "The bus's coming, I hear the motorbus!"

"Lying won't help you. I was savin' that bottle for a special occasion, and you filched it outa my—" LeRoy stopped, staring toward the plaza, where the growling whine of the approaching bus was coming. "You're right, it is. But you just wait, Em. . . ."

They hastened into the plaza, just as the dust-matted Great Southwestern Autocoach rocked into view around a bend in the road. Even more so than in Canta Lupe, its arrival in Valle was a major event to break the day's monotony, and bystanders gathered about to regard its every move as the motorbus shuddered to a halt in front of the long building. The driver opened the door but kept the engine running; Valle was not considered a stop, but a pause.

The four men climbed on and showed their tickets. The bus rumbled and snorted, picking up speed, and the men swayed as they shuffled down the narrow aisle, peering in the dimness for seats.

"Matt!" a familiar voice gasped. Then another. "Guffy!"

Startled, the men moved to the rear, where Heloise and Aurora were sitting together. Aurora slid across the aisle, so that Guffy could sit with her and Matt with Heloise, and Shelby and Crandon shifted into the seats just in front of them.

Bishop answered Heloise's look. "Your car broke down."

"Oh, I'm sorry. But at least you got away, that's good." She leaned against his shoulder. "Aren't you surprised to see me?"

"Naw."

"You liar." She gazed at him, lips framing words she didn't speak, and then she lowered her eyes. "You were going to Tucson, we remembered Em saying that. When Aurora suggested a . . . shopping trip, I thought, why not? I've already been dealing with the enemy."

"So you figured you might as well switch sides, eh?"

She looked at him again, the window haloing her hair, the spill of sunset highlighting her freckled nose. "Yes," she said softly, her tongue moistening her lips. "If you wish . . . yes."

Bishop grinned, but didn't reply. He leaned across the aisle, glancing past LeRoy to Aurora, who was wedged in her seat with a cloth traveling bag perched on her expansive lap. When she'd finished saying something to Guffy, he asked her, "How'd it go at the bank?"

"I was just telling Guffy, it worked like magic. A bunch of hotheads were already pressing Junius, not even waiting until he was decently dressed. So I handed him my money and said, 'Deposit this, it's safer here than with me, and earns good interest to boot.' "

LeRoy laughed. "Bet he wondered plenty where you got it."

"No, he was too relieved to have it for withdrawals. When the worst o' the blowhards got theirs, the others started realizing they were being silly and left, and the run was squelched before it could start. Afterward, I told Junius my money was to pay off the rest of my mortgage, not just my next payment. Told him I was selling out the Northern Lights, and it'd come from the buyer who'd wanted clear title." She folded her arms across the bag. "Think I will sell, too."

"Don't be hasty," LeRoy advised. "You've a tidy business."

"Not a proper one, though, for a respectable married lady."

"Mar–! Damnit, who is he? Who's the rat you're hitching?"

"Why care?" She sighed tremulously. "You never asked me."

"I . . . I would've, maybe! Except, ah, it ain't proper for no gent, neither, not to be able to support a wife, and I've always been tapped, like now. If you hadn't gone 'n' returned Junius all our loot–"

"Guffy LeRoy, you got tin ears too? We had to save the bank, and my place got saved in doing so. But whoever said anything about having to save all of Junius's skin?" She unlatched the cloth bag and dug out a fistful of cash. "Best we can calc'late, Junius is still in arrears about eighteen thousand dollars. Now ask me again, sweetums!"

LeRoy boogered. "I've done been skunked!"

Chuckling, Bishop turned back to Heloise. He placed a callused palm against her cheek, caressing gently, tenderly. "Never mind what I wish. It's like I was saying before, you've gotta act on your own wantin' and needin'. You've gotta take the responsibility for 'em."

"I am. I have." She pressed her hand over his, drawing his down to her lips, and he felt the warmth of her mouth nuzzling his fingertips. "I left Junius on my own. I got on this bus not knowing if you'd been caught, if I'd see you again or what you'd do if I did."

N23 "I just have to be sure you don't expect my wishin' to be your excuse," he said. "I make a lousy leanin' post, and . . ."

He trailed off with a slight sucking in of his breath. Outside the window by Heloise, he'd spotted a line of four black touring cars chugging past the bus. Stern-faced men were squeezed in front and rear, some with rifles and shotguns propped upright between their legs. And Bishop didn't need to lean out the window and ask them to know that there'd be badges pinned underneath their somber suit jackets.

"Lawdogs," Crandon muttered, staring out his window.

"Sniffin' our trail," Shelby added, peering across him.

Drawing, LeRoy spun the cylinder of his revolver. "Good thing we didn't waste lead firing our peashooters at Deputy Max."

"Not here, Guffy," Bishop said. "Not with the women."

Tensely he watched the cars slowly file alongside. The driver of the third happened to glance up, and for a startling instant, Bishop thought he recognized old Timotheus Tighe. The same moustache, the same square face, the same cold gray eyes. . . . But it wasn't Tighe, of course, just the resemblance of him, the image of what he represented. The row continued, rumbling on and disappearing in their own dust.

Bishop sat back, suddenly limp. "Never again, I swear."

"That was something else you were telling me, wasn't it?" Heloise cupped his hand in her lap now, her gaze searching, haunting. "Learn from the past but look to the future, wasn't that the gist of it? Otherwise we keep going back and repeating our same mistakes?"

"Yeah, that's about it." He studied her for a long moment, sensing surrender inside him—feeling his old faith reviving, his blind love resuming. Strange, he thought; despite his best advice, he was willingly repeating his own past. "But on occasion," he added in a whisper, "on occasion going back ain't such a bad mistake."

He embraced her then with his other hand, drawing Heloise close till her head touched his chest. Facing frontward, Bishop rested his cheek lightly against the crown of her hair.

"But goddamned if I'm going to return again, not never!"

ABOUT THE AUTHORS

Thomas Jeier lives in Germany, where he works for a publishing company. *Jeffrey M. Wallmann* lives in Eugene, Oregon. Both are members of the Western Writers of America.